Welcome to Harlequin's great new series,
created by some of our bestselling authors
from Down Under:

THE AUSTRALIANS

Twelve tales of heated romance and adventure—
guaranteed to turn your whole world upside down!

Travel to an Outback cattle station, experience the
glamour of the Gold Coast or visit the bright lights
of Sydney where you'll meet twelve engaging young
women, all feisty and all about to face their biggest
challenge yet...falling in love.

And it will take some very special women to tame
our heroes! Strong, rugged, often infuriating and
always irresistible, they're one hundred percent prime
Australian male: hard to get close to...but even
harder to forget!

The Wonder from Down Under:
where spirited women win the hearts of
Australia's most independent men.

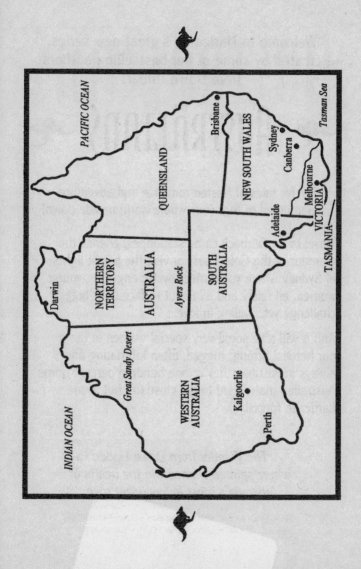

THE
AUSTRALIANS

SIMPLY
IRRESISTIBLE

Miranda Lee

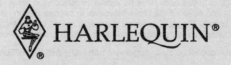

TORONTO • NEW YORK • LONDON
AMSTERDAM • PARIS • SYDNEY • HAMBURG
STOCKHOLM • ATHENS • TOKYO • MILAN • MADRID
PRAGUE • WARSAW • BUDAPEST • AUCKLAND

ISBN 0-373-82584-6

SIMPLY IRRESISTIBLE

First North American Publication 1999.

Printed in U.S.A.

Miranda Lee is Australian, living near Sydney. Born and raised in the bush, she was boarding-school educated and briefly pursued a classical music career before moving to Sydney and embracing the world of computers. Happily married, with three daughters, she began writing when family commitments kept her at home. She has written over thirty books for the Harlequin Presents® series, and likes to create stories that are believable, modern, fast paced and sexy. Her interests include reading meaty sagas, doing word puzzles, gambling and going to the movies.

CHAPTER ONE

'WE'VE been accused of doing too many heavy stories lately,' Mervyn announced to his underlings seated around the oval table. 'From now on, one of the four segments we tape for each week's show is going to be in a lighter vein.'

Vivien looked up from where she was doodling on her note-pad, a sinking feeling in her stomach. As the last reporter to join the *Across Australia* team—not to mention the only woman—she just *knew* who would be assigned these 'lighter-veined' stories.

She hadn't long come off a *Candid Camera* style programme, and while it had been a huge success, she'd been relieved to finally have the chance to work on a television show that was more intellectually stimulating. At twenty-five going on twenty-six, she felt she was old enough to be taken seriously.

Ah, well, she sighed. One step forward and two steps backwards...

'And what constitutes lighter-veined?' demanded a male voice from across the table.

Vivien glanced over at Bob, widely known as Robert J. Overhill, their hard-hitting political reporter who wouldn't know 'lighter-veined' if it hit him in the left eye. Thirtyish, but already going bald and running to fat, he conducted every interview as a personal war out of which he *had* to emerge the victor. He had a sharp, incisive mind, but the personality of a spoilt little boy.

'I'm not sure myself yet,' Mervyn returned. 'This directive has just come down from the great white chief himself. I've only had time to think up a try-out idea to be screened on Sunday week. Ever heard of Wallaby Creek?' he queried with a wry grin on his intelligent face.

They all shook their heads.

'It's a small town out in north-western New South Wales just this side of Bourke, but off the main highway. Once a year, in the middle of November, it's where the Outback Shearers' Association hold their Bachelors' and Spinsters' Ball.'

Everyone rolled their eyes as the penny dropped. There'd been a current affairs programme done on a similar B & S Ball a couple of years before, which had depicted the event as a drunken orgy filled with loutish yobbos and female desperadoes. The only claim to dubious fame the event seemed to have was that no girl went home a virgin.

Vivien chuckled to herself at the thought that, from what she had seen, not too many virgins had gone to that particular ball in the first place.

'I'm so glad you find the idea an amusing one, Viv,' her producer directed straight at her, 'since you'll be handling it. The ball's this Saturday night. That gives you three days to get yourself organised and out there. Now I'm not interested in any serious message in this story. Just a fun piece. Froth and bubble. Right?'

Vivien diplomatically kept her chagrin to herself. 'Right,' she said, and threw a bright smile around the table at all the smug male faces smirking at her.

It never ceased to amaze her, the pleasure men got from seeing women supposedly put in their places in the workplace, but she had always found the best line of defence was to be agreeable, rather than militant. She defused any antagonism with feminine charm, then counter-attacked by always giving her very best, doing such a damn good job—even with froth and bubble—that her male colleagues had to give her some credit.

'I hear they drink pretty heavily at those balls,' Bob said in a mocking tone. 'We might have to send out a search party of trackers to find Viv the next day. You know what she's like after a couple of glasses. Whew...' He whistled and waved his hand in front of his face, as though he was suddenly very hot.

Vivien sighed while the others laughed. Would she *never* live down the channel's Christmas party last year? How was she to know that someone had spiked the supposedly non-alcoholic fruit punch with vodka? She was always so careful when it came to drinking, ever since she'd discovered several years before at her first university party that anything more than two glasses of the mildest concoction turned her from a quietly spoken, serious-minded girl into a flamboyant exhibitionist, not to mention a rather outrageous flirt.

Luckily for Vivien on that first occasion, her girlfriend had dragged her home before she got herself into any serious trouble. But her hangover the next morning, plus the stark memory of her silly and potentially dangerous behaviour, had made her very careful with alcohol from that moment on.

The incident at last year's Christmas party had hardly been her fault. Vivien groaned silently as she recalled how, once the alcohol took effect, she'd actually climbed up on this very table and danced a wild tango, complete with a rose in her mouth.

Earl had been furious with her, dragging her down and taking her home post-haste. He'd hardly spoken to her for a week. It had taken much longer for the people at work to stop making pointed remarks over the incident. Now, her acid-tongued colleague had brought it up again. Still, Vivien knew the worst thing she could do would be to react visibly.

'Worried you might miss out on something, Bob?' she countered with a light laugh.

'Hardly,' he scowled. 'I like my women a touch less aggressive.'

'Cut it out, Bob,' Mervyn intervened before the situation flared out of hand. 'Oh, and Viv, I can only let you have a single-man crew. You like working that way anyway, don't you?'

'I'll get Irving,' she said. Irving was a peach to work with, a whiz with camera and sound. A witty companion, too.

But the best part about Irving was that he wasn't a womaniser and never tried to chat her up. In his late twenties, he had a steady girlfriend who adored him and whom he adored back. Fidelity was his middle name. Definitely Vivien's type of man.

'It goes without saying that you'll both have to drive out. *And* in the same car,' Mervyn went on. 'You know how tight things have been since they cut our budget again. I rang the one and only hotel in Wallaby Creek to see if they had any vacancies and, luckily enough, they did. Seems the proprietor is refusing to house any revellers for the ball after a couple of his rooms were almost wrecked last year. Might I suggest you don't leave any valuable equipment in the car that night after you've retired? OK?'

'Sure thing, boss,' Vivien agreed. Maybe it wouldn't be so bad, she decided philosophically. She'd always wanted to drive out west for a look-see, having never been beyond the Blue Mountains. Not that she secretly hankered for a country lifestyle. Vivien was a Sydney girl. Born and bred. She couldn't see herself giving up the vibrant hustle and bustle of city life for wide-open spaces, dust and flies.

Not only that, but it would give her something to do this weekend, since Earl didn't want her to fly down to visit him. *Once again*, she reminded herself with a jab of dismay.

'Well, off you go, madam,' her boss announced before depression could take hold. 'Grab Irving before he's booked up elsewhere. That man's in high demand.'

'Right.' She smiled, and stood up.

'Phone call for you, Vivien,' the main receptionist called out to her as she passed through the foyer area on her way back to her office. 'I'll switch it back to your desk now. That is where you're heading, isn't it? It's STD, by the way. Your boyfriend.'

Vivien's heart skipped a beat. *Earl*? Ringing her during working hours? That wasn't like him at all...

She hurried along the corridor towards the office she shared with her three fellow *Across Australia* reporters, her heart pounding with sudden nerves.

Somehow she just knew this phone call didn't mean what she so desperately hoped it meant, that Earl wanted to say sorry for the way he'd been behaving, that he was missing her as much as she was missing him. Perhaps he'd finally given up trying to make her suffer for not dropping her career and following him to Melbourne the second he got his promotion and transfer six weeks ago.

Her heart twisted as she recalled the awful argument they'd had when he'd come home that night and made his impossible demand. She'd tried explaining that if she just quit on the spot she'd be committing professional suicide. But he hadn't been prepared to listen, his relentlessly cold logic being that if she loved him she would do what *he* wanted, what was best for *him*. If she wanted to marry him and have his children, then *her* career was irrelevant.

Although he had always shown chauvinistic tendencies, his stubborn selfishness in this matter had startled then infuriated her. She had dug in her heels and stayed in Sydney. Nevertheless, she had still been prepared to compromise, promising to look for a position in Melbourne in the New Year, which had been only three months away. To which idea Earl had sulkily agreed.

To begin with, Vivien had flown to Melbourne every weekend to be with him. These visits, however, had not been a great success, with the old argument inevitably flaring about her throwing in her job and staying with him. After three weeks of these bitter-sweet reunions, Earl had started finding reasons for her not to come, saying he was busy with one thing and another. Which perhaps he was… But underneath, Vivien believed he'd been exacting a type of revenge on her, being petty in a way he'd never been before.

She swept into the empty office and over to her corner,

sending papers flying as she slid on to the corner of her desk and snatched up the receiver.

'Hello?' she said breathlessly.

'Vivien? That is you, isn't it?' Earl drawled in a voice she scarcely recognised.

Taken aback, she was lost for words for a moment. Where on earth had he got that accent from? He sounded like an upper-class snob, yet he was from a working-class background, just like herself.

'Oh—er—yes, it's me,' she finally blurted out.

His laugh had the most peculiarly dry note to it. 'You sound rattled. Have I caught you doing things you shouldn't be doing with all those men you work with?'

Now *that* was just like Earl. Jealous as sin.

She suppressed an unhappy sigh. He didn't have to be jealous. She'd never given him a moment's doubt over her loyalty from the moment she'd fallen in love with him two years before. Hadn't she even gone against her principles and agreed to live with him when he postponed their plans to marry till he was thirty?

'Don't be silly, darling,' she cajoled. 'You know you're the only man for me.'

'Do I? I'm not so sure, Vivien. And *you're* the one who's been silly. *Very* silly.'

Vivien was chilled by the tone in his voice.

'If you'd just come with me when I asked you to,' he continued peevishly, 'none of this would have happened.'

'None of w—what would have happened?' she asked, a sick feeling starting in the pit of her stomach.

'We'd probably be married by now,' he raved on, totally ignoring her tremulous question. 'The chairman of the bank down here likes his executives suitably spoused.

You would have been perfect for the role of my wife, Vivien, with your personality and looks. But *no*! You had to have your own career as well, didn't you? You had to be liberated! Well, consider yourself liberated, my sweet. Set free, free of everything, including me.'

Vivien thought she made a choking, gasping sound. But perhaps she didn't.

'Besides, I've met someone else,' he pronounced with a bald cruelty that took her breath away. 'She's the daughter of a well-connected businessman down here. Not as stunning-looking as you, I admit. But then, not many women are,' he added caustically. 'But she's prepared to be a full-time wife, to devote herself entirely to *me*!'

Shock was sending Vivien's head into a spin. She wanted to drop the phone. Run. Anything. This couldn't be happening to her. Earl *couldn't* be telling her he'd found someone else, some woman he was going to *marry*?

Somehow she gathered herself with a strength that was perhaps only illusory. But she clung to it all the same.

'Earl,' she said with a quiet desperation, 'I love you. And I know you love me. Don't do this to us...not...not for the sake of ambition.'

'Ambition?' he scoffed. 'You *dare* talk to me of ambition? You, who put your career ahead of your so-called love for me? Don't make me laugh, sweetheart. Actually, I consider myself lucky to be getting out from under this...*obsession* I had for you. Any man would find it hard to give you up. But I'm cured now. I've kicked the habit. And I have my methadone at hand.' He laughed. 'Name of Amelia.'

Vivien was dimly aware that she was now in danger of cracking up on the spot. The hand that was clutching the receiver to her ear was going cold, shivers reverberating up her arm. She tried to speak, but couldn't.

'I'll be up this Saturday to get the rest of my things,' Earl continued callously. 'I'd like you to be conspicuously absent. Visit your folks or something. Oh, for pity's sake, say something, Vivien! You're beginning to bore me with this frozen silence routine. It's positively childish. You must have known the writing was on the wall once you refused to come with me.'

'I...I would have come,' she said in an emotionally devastated voice, 'if I'd known this would happen. Earl, please...I *love* you—'

'No, you bloody well don't,' he shot back nastily. 'No more than I loved you. I can see now it was only lust. I'm surprised it lasted as long as it did.'

Only lust?

Her face flamed with humiliation and hurt. She couldn't count the number of times sex hadn't been all that good for her. She'd merely pretended. For *his* sake. For his infernal male pride!

'No come-backs?' he jeered. 'Fine. I don't want to argue, either. After all, there's nothing really to argue about. You made your choice, Vivien. Now you can damned well live with it!' And he slammed down the phone.

She stared down at the dead receiver, her mind reeling as the reality of the situation hit her.

Earl was gone from her life.

Not just temporarily.

Forever.

All her plans for the future—shattered.

There would be no marriage to him. No children by him. No nothing.

Tears welled up behind her eyes and she might have buried her face in her hands and sobbed her heart out had not Robert J. Overhill appeared in the doorway of the office at that precise moment. Luckily his sharp eyes didn't go to her pale, shaken face. They zeroed in on her long, shapely legs dangling over the desk corner.

For the first time Vivien understood Bob's vicious attitude towards her. He *did* fancy her, her crime being that she didn't fancy him back.

With a desperate burst of pride she kept the tears at bay. 'Well!' She jumped to her feet and plastered a bright smile on her face. 'I'd better stop this lounging about and get to work. You wouldn't know where Irving might be, would you?'

'Haven't a clue.' Bob shrugged, his narrowed eyes travelling slowly back up her body.

'I'll try the canteen,' she said breezily.

'You do that.'

He remained standing in the narrow doorway so that she had to turn sideways and brush past him to leave the room, her full breasts connecting with his arm.

But she said, 'Excuse me,' airily as though it didn't matter, and hurried up the corridor, hiding the shudder that ran deeply through her. All of a sudden, she hated men. The whole breed. For they were indeed hateful creatures, she decided. Hateful! Incapable of true love. Incapable of caring. All they thought about or wanted was sex.

But then she remembered her father. Her sweet, kind, loving father. And her two older brothers. Both good men with stable, secure marriages and happy wives and families. Even Irving was loyal and true, and *he* was in the television industry, hardly a hotbed of faithfulness. Was she asking for too much to want that kind of man for herself?

'Oh, Irving!' she called out, spotting the man himself leaving the canteen.

He spun round and smiled at her. 'What's up, Doc?'

'Got a job for you.'

'Thank the lord it's you and not Bob. I've had politicians up to here!' And he drew a line across his throat. 'So where are we off to this time?'

'Ever heard of Wallaby Creek?'

CHAPTER TWO

THE Wallaby Creek hotel was typical of hotels found in bush towns throughout Australia.

It was two-storeyed and quite roomy, sporting a corrugated-iron roof—painted green—and wooden verandas all around, the upper one with iron lacework railings—painted cream. It sat on the inevitable corner, so that any patrons who cared to wander out from their upstairs room on to the adjoining veranda would be guaranteed a splendid view of the main street below and an unimpeded panorama for miles around.

Vivien was standing on this veranda at six on the following Saturday evening, wiping the perspiration from her neck and looking out in awe at the incredible scene still taking shape before her eyes.

When she and Irving had driven into the small, dusty town the previous evening, tired and hot from the day-long trip west, they'd wondered where the ball would be held, since, at first glance, Wallaby Creek consisted of little else but this hotel, a few ancient houses, a general store and two garages.

They'd asked the hotel proprietor, a jolly soul named Bert, if there was a hall they'd missed. He'd given a good belly-laugh and told them no, no hall, then refused to answer their next query as to where the venue for the ball would be.

'Just you wait and see,' he'd chuckled. 'Come tomorrow afternoon, you won't recognise this place.'

He'd been right. In the short space of a few hours, the sleepy hollow of Wallaby Creek had been transformed.

First, heavy-transport vehicles accompanied by utilities filled with men had descended on the place like a plague of locusts, and within a short while a marquee that would have done the Russian circus proud had mushroomed in a nearby paddock. Next came the dance-floor, square slabs of wooden decking that fitted together like giant parquet.

A car park was then marked out with portable fences, its size showing that they were anticipating an exceptionally large turn-out. This expectation was reinforced by the two long lines of porta-loos that stretched out on either side of the marquee, one marked 'Chicks', the other 'Blokes'.

Refreshment vans had rolled into town all day, with everything from meat pies to champagne to kegs of beer. Two enormous barbecues had been set up on either side of the front entrance to the marquee, complete with a multitude of plastic tables and chairs, not to mention plastic glasses and cutlery. Lessons had been learnt, it seemed, from accidents in previous years. Real glass was out!

Vivien had been kept busy all day, interviewing all sorts of people, from the members of the organising committee to the volunteers who helped put the venue together to the people who hoped to make a quick buck out of hot dogs or steak sandwiches or what have you.

She was amazed at the distance some of the men had travelled, though it had been patiently explained to her that Wallaby Creek was fairly central to most of the sheep properties around this section of New South Wales and country people were used to covering vast distances for their entertainment. Every unmarried jackeroo, rouse-about, stockhand and shearer in a three-hundred-kilometre radius would be in attendance tonight, she was assured, together with a sprinkling of station owners and other assorted B & S Ball fans. Apparently a few carloads of young ladies even drove out from Sydney for such occasions, in search of a man.

If Vivien hadn't been so depressed inside, she might have been caught up in the general air of excited anticipation that seemed to be pervading everyone. But she couldn't even get up enough enthusiasm to start getting ready. Instead, she lingered outside, leaning on the old iron railing, staring at the horizon, which was bathed in the bold reds and golds of an outback sunset.

But she was blind to the raw, rich beauty of the land, her mind back in her flat in Sydney, where at this very moment Earl was probably taking away every single reminder she had of him. When she went back, it would almost be as though he had never existed.

Only he *had* existed, she moaned silently. And would continue to exist in her mind and heart for a long, long time.

Vivien's hands lifted to wipe moisture away from her eyes.

Damn, she thought abruptly. I can't possibly be crying again. There can't be any tears left! Angry with herself, she spun away and strode inside into the hotel room. 'No more,' she muttered, and swept up the towels off the bed for a quick visit to the bathroom. 'No more!'

And she didn't cry any more. But she still suffered, her heart heavy in her chest at having thought about Earl again, her normally sparkling eyes flat and dull as she went about transforming herself as astonishingly and speedily as Wallaby Creek had been.

By five to seven, the miracle was almost complete. Gone were the pale blue cotton trousers and simple white shirt she'd been wearing all day, replaced by a strapless ball-gown and matching bolero in a deep purple taffeta. Down was her thick black hair, dancing around her shoulders and face in soft, glossy waves. On had gone her night-time make-up, dramatic and bold, putting a high blush of colour across her smooth alabaster cheeks, turning her already striking brown eyes into even darker pools of exotic mystery, emphasising her sensually wide mouth with a coating of shimmering violet gloss.

At last Vivien stood back to give herself a cynical appraisal in the old dressing-table mirror. Now who are you trying to look so sensational for, you fool? And she shook her head at herself in mockery.

Still, the dressy dress was a must, since all patrons of the ball were required to wear formal clothes. And one did look insipid on television at night unless well made up.

There was a rapid knocking on her door. 'Viv? Are you ready?' Irving asked.

'Coming,' she said brusquely, and, slipping her bare feet into high-heeled black sandals, she swept from the room.

By ten the ball was in full swing, the heavy-metal band that had been brought up from Sydney blaring out its strident beat to a packed throng of energetic dancers. Vivien squeezed a path between the heaving, weaving bodies with her microphone and cameraman in tow, doing fleeting interviews as she went, as well as a general commentary that she probably wouldn't use except as a basis for her final voice-over.

Most of the merry-makers were co-operative and tolerant, and when she remarked to one group that some of the young people's 'formal' gear was not of the best quality she'd been laughingly told that 'experienced' B & S Ball attendees always purchased their tuxes and gowns from second-hand clothing establishments.

'Otherwise their good clothes might get ruined!' One young man winked.

'How?' she asked.

They all looked at her as though she'd just descended from Mars.

'In the creek, of course! Don't you city folks have creeks down in Sydney?'

'Er—well…' Hard to explain that one didn't go swimming in the Parramatta or St. George's River. Too much pollution. 'We do have the harbour,' she tried.

'Not as good as our creek,' someone said, and they all laughed knowingly.

They were still laughing as she moved on.

'I'm getting hot and tired, Viv,' Irving said shortly before eleven. 'I could do with a bite to eat and a cool drink.'

It was indeed becoming stuffy in the marquee and Vivien herself fancied a breath of fresh air. 'OK. Meet me back here, near the band, at midnight,' she suggested.

'Will do. Here. Give me the mike.' He rolled up the cord, slung it over his shoulder with his camera, and in seconds had disappeared, swallowed up by the throng.

Suddenly, despite being in the middle of a mêlée,

Vivien felt incredibly lonely. With a weary sigh she glanced around, waffling over which of the various exits she would make for, and it was as her eyes were skating over the bobbing heads of dancers that she got the shock of her life.

For there was Earl, leaning against one of the tent poles, looking very elegant in a black evening suit, bow-tie and all.

She gasped, her view of him obscured for a moment. But when the intervening couples moved out of the way again she realised it wasn't Earl at all, but a man with a face and hair so similar to Earl's that it was scary.

She couldn't help staring at him, and as she stared his eyes slowly turned, drawn no doubt by her intense scrutiny. And then he was looking right at her.

The breath was punched from her lungs. God, but he was the spitting image of Earl! Facially, at least.

Perhaps she should have looked away, now that he was aware of her regard. But she couldn't seem to. It was as though she were hypnotised by this man's uncanny resemblance to the man who had been her lover for the past two years.

A frown formed on his handsome face as they exchanged stares, an oddly troubled frown. It struck Vivien that perhaps he thought he was getting the come-on and was embarrassed by her none too subtle stare.

But if he was, why didn't he just look away?

Suddenly, he moved—destroying his almost apparition-like quality—his spine straightening, his shoulders squaring inside his black dinner-jacket. His eyes never left her.

He was walking now, moving inexorably towards her, the gyrating crowd parting before him like the Red Sea

had for Moses. Closer, he was still incredibly like Earl.
The way his thick brown hair swept across his forehead
from a side parting. The wide, sensuous mouth. And that
damned dimple in the middle of a similarly strong square-
cut jaw.

But he was taller and leaner than Earl. And his eyes
weren't grey. They were a light ice-blue. They were also
compellingly fixed on her as he loomed closer and closer.

Vivien's big brown eyes flicked over his elegant dinner
suit. No second-hand rubbish for him, she thought, and
swallowed nervously. Jackets didn't fit like that unless
they were individually tailored. Of course, he was no cal-
low youth either. He had to be at least thirty.

He stopped right in front of her, a slow and vaguely
sardonic smile coming to his face. 'Care to dance?' he
asked in a voice like dark chocolate.

'D-dance?' She blinked up at him, thrown by how
amazingly similar that lop-sided, lazy smile was to Earl's.

His smile grew wider, thankfully destroying the likeness. 'Yes, dance. You know...two people with arms
around each other, moving in unison.'

She blushed under his teasing, which rattled her even
more than his looks. Good grief, she *never* blushed, having achieved a measure of fame around the channel for
her sophisticated composure, her ability never to be
thrown by anything or anyone. Which was perhaps why
everyone had been so surprised by the wildly mad exhi-
bition she had made of herself at that Christmas party.

'I...yes...all right,' she answered, her mind in chaos,
her heart pounding away in her chest like a jackhammer.

He swept her smoothly into his arms and away on to
the dance-floor, and once again there seemed to be mi-

raculous room for him. She felt light as a feather in his arms. 'I don't disco,' he murmured, pulling her to him and pressing soft lips into her hair. 'I like my women close.'

'Oh,' was all she could manage in reply.

Good lord, she thought. What am I *doing*? I should have said no. He *had* to have got the wrong idea from my none too subtle staring, not to mention my tongue-tied schoolgirl reaction to his invitation.

Make your apologies and extricate yourself before things get awkward here, she advised herself.

Yet she stayed right where she was and said absolutely nothing, aware of little but the pounding of her heart and the feeling of excitement that was racing through her veins.

Somehow Earl's double invented a dance to the primitive beat of the music, even though it was more a rhythmic swaying than any real movement across the floor. People swirled back around them, shutting them in, making Vivien feel suddenly tight-chested and claustrophic. Someone knocked into them and her partner pulled her even closer, flattening her breasts against the hard wall of his chest.

'Put your arms up around my neck,' he murmured. 'You'll be less of a target that way.'

True, she thought breathlessly. I'll also probably cease to exist as a separate entity, because if I get any closer I'll have become part of *you*!

But she did as he suggested, amazed at herself for her easy acquiescence. The whole situation had a weird, supernatural feel to it, from the man's uncanny likeness to Earl to her out-of-character reactions to him.

Or maybe they were *in* character, she thought dazedly. Maybe her body was simply responding to the same physical chemistry she felt when she was with Earl. Her responses were not really for this man. They were merely for a face, the face of the man she loved.

A moan of dismay punched which sounded more sensual than desolate from her throat and clearly gave her partner even more of the right—or wrong—idea.

'You feel it too, don't you?' he rasped, one of his hands sliding up under her bolero to trace erotic circles over her naked shoulder blades. 'Incredible…'

She tensed in his arms, appalled yet fascinated by her own arousal. She couldn't seem to gather the courage or common sense to pull away, to put a stop to what was happening between them. When he bent his head to kiss her neck, a betraying shiver of pleasure rippled through her. He groaned, opening his mouth to suckle softly at her flesh.

A compulsive wave of desire broke the last of her control and her fingers began to steal up into his silky, thick hair, fingertips pressing into his scalp.

'God…' he muttered against her neck.

The mindless depth of arousal in his voice plus an abrupt appreciation of where they actually were acted like a cold sponge on Vivien, snapping her back to reality.

'Dear heaven,' she cried, and, shuddering with shame, wrenched away from him.

He stared down at her, smouldering blue eyes still glazed with passion.

Her left hand fluttered up to agitatedly touch her neck where his mouth had been. The skin felt hot and wet and rough. There had to be a red mark. 'You shouldn't have done that,' she burst out. 'I...I didn't like it.'

A chill came into his eyes. 'Didn't you?'

'No, of...of course not!' she denied, her demeanour as flustered as his was now composed.

His eyes narrowed, his top lip curling with a type of sardonic contempt. 'So,' he said with a dry laugh, 'you're nothing but a tease. How ironic. How bloody ironic.'

For a moment she stared back up at him, confused by his words. But then she was angry. 'No, I'm *not*!' she retorted, chin lifting defiantly. 'And there's no need to swear!'

But when she went to whirl away his hand shot out to grab her arm, spinning her back into his body. 'Then *why*?' he flung at her in a low, husky voice. 'Why look at me the way you did? Why let me go that far before you stopped me?'

What could she say? I don't know? Maybe it wasn't *you* I was letting do that. Maybe it wasn't *you* I was wanting.

And yet...

She stared into the depths of the eyes, looking for answers, but finding only more confusion. For suddenly Earl was the furthest thing from her mind.

'You...you wouldn't understand,' she muttered.

'Wouldn't I? Try me.' And he gathered her forcefully back into his arms.

She gaped up at him. But before she could voice any bewildered protest he urged her back into their rocking, rolling rhythm, his hold firm, his eyes stubborn. 'Start explaining.'

For a second, her hands pushed at his immutable shoulders. But it was like trying to push a brick wall down with a feather.

'I deserve an explanation,' he said with maddening logic. 'So stop that nonsense and give me one.'

She glared up at him, knowing she should demand he let go of her, should tell him he had no right to use his superior male strength to enforce his will. Yet all she wanted was to close her eyes and melt back into him. It was incredible!

'I don't think I'm asking too much, do you?' he went on, disarming her with a wry but warm smile.

She groaned in defeat, her forehead tipping forwards on to his rock-hard chest. When he actually picked up her arms and put them around his neck, she glanced up at him, then wished she hadn't. He was too overwhelmingly close and too disturbingly attractive to her.

'So tell me,' he murmured. 'Why did you stare at me the way you did?'

Vivien tried to think of a plausible lie, but couldn't. How could she explain something she didn't fully understand herself? With considerable reluctance, she was forced to embrace the part she *could* grasp. 'When I first saw you I thought you were someone else. You...you look a lot like someone I know. *Used* to know,' she amended.

'An old boyfriend?'

'Sort of.'

He pulled back slightly and gave her a penetrating look. 'Would you like to be more specific?'

She sighed. 'Ex-lover, then.'

'How ex is ex? A week? A month? A year?'

'Three days. *No.*' She laughed bitterly. 'Three *weeks*. Maybe even longer. I just didn't know till three days ago.'

He stopped dancing. There was a strange stillness about his body.

'I see,' he finally exhaled, and began to move again.

'What about later?' he resumed casually enough. 'When we started to dance? What's your excuse for that?'

'I can't explain it,' she choked out.

'Neither can I,' he said, the hand on her waist lifting to hold the back of her head with surprising tenderness, forcing her face to nestle under his chin. 'I've never felt anything like it. Yet I don't even know your name.'

'Vivien,' she whispered, her lips dangerously close to his throat.

'Vivien what?'

'Roberts.'

'Mine's Ross. Ross Everton.'

'Are...are you a shearer?' she asked, trying desperately to get their conversation on to safe, neutral territory. Anything to defuse the physical tension still enveloping her.

'I *can* shear. But it's not my main job.'

She pulled her mouth away from his neck and looked up. 'Which is?'

'I manage a sheep station.'

'I would have thought you were an owner.'

He arched one of his eyebrows. 'Why's that?'

'You don't sound like a shearer or a jackeroo.' Which he didn't. He sounded very well educated.

He laughed. 'And what are they supposed to sound like? I'll have you know we had a jackeroo on our place last year who was the son of an English lord.'

'*Our* place? I thought you said you managed.'

'I do. My father's property. For the moment, that is.'

'You sound as if it's only a temporary arrangement.'

A black cloud passed over those piercing blue eyes. 'Dad had a serious stroke last month. The doctors say his chances of having another fatal one are high.'

'Oh. I…I'm sorry.'

'It's all right. You couldn't have known.'

There was a short, sharp silence between them.

'So tell me, Vivien Roberts,' he said abruptly. 'What television programme are you representing here tonight? No, don't bother asking. I spotted you earlier doing your stuff. Is it *Country Wide*? The *Investigators*, maybe? As you can see, we country folk can watch any station we like as long as it's the ABC.'

She laughed, and felt her tension lessen. 'Sorry, but I'm from a disgusting commercial station and the show's called *Across Australia*. And if you tell me you've never heard of it I'll be mortified.'

'I've heard of it,' he admitted, 'but never seen it. Do you think I'd forget you, if I had?'

Her stomach flipped over at the intensity he managed to put into what should have been a casual compliment.

'Ross,' she began hesitantly, 'this…this attraction between us. It can't go anywhere.'

Again she felt that stilling in his body. 'Why not?'

'It…it wouldn't be fair to you.'

'In what way?'

What could she say? Because you're not just *like* the man I've loved and lost. You're almost his mirror image. I'd never know if what I felt for you was real or not.

Besides, you're from a different world from me, a world I would never fit into or want to fit into.

'I'm still in love with Earl,' she said, thinking that should answer all arguments.

Ross was irritatingly silent for ages before saying, 'I presume Earl is the man I remind you of, your ex-lover?'

'Yes,' was her reluctant admission.

His laugh sounded odd. 'Even more ironic. Tell me honestly, Vivien, if dear Earl walked back into your life this minute would you take him back?'

'Never!'

'That sounded promisingly bitter. Didn't he love you?'

'I thought he did. Apparently not, however. He's moved to Melbourne and found someone else.'

'I presume you're from Sydney, then?'

'You presume right.'

'And you're going to take your broken heart and enter a convent, is that it?'

Startled, she stared up at him. There was a mocking light in his eyes.

'Very funny,' she bit out.

'Yes, it would be. Somehow I don't think the woman I held in my arms a few minutes back would make a very good nun.'

She might have wrenched herself out of his arms and stalked away at that point if they hadn't been interrupted by a third party, a good-looking young man who tapped Ross on the shoulder with one hand while he held a can of beer in the other. By the look of him, it hadn't been his first drink of the night.

'Well, well, well,' he drawled with a drunken slur. 'I thought you were supposed to be here to watch over me, big brother. But *I've* been watching *you*. What would our dear father think of his God-like first son if I told him you spent this evening so differently from the rest of us mortal men, trying to get into some woman's knickers?'

Vivien gasped, then gasped again when Ross's fist flew out, connecting with his brother's chin. For a second, the young man merely looked shocked, swaying back and forth on his heels. But then his bloodshot eyes rolled back into his head and he tipped backwards, his fall broken by the quick reflexes of the man he'd just insulted.

'Well, don't just stand there, Vivien,' Ross grated out, looking up from where he was bent over his brother, hands hooked under his armpits. 'Pick up his feet and help me get the silly idiot out into some fresh air!'

CHAPTER THREE

No ONE seemed particularly concerned as Ross and Vivien carted the unconscious young man through the crowd towards the front exit.

'Too much to drink, eh?' was the only comment they received.

Vivien began to think one could murder someone here tonight and get away with it, by saying the corpse was 'dead' drunk as it was carried off for disposal.

'For a lightly built young man, he's darned heavy,' she complained once they made it out of the marquee and tried to prop him up in one of the plastic chairs. Vivien frowned as his head flopped forwards on to his chest. 'Do you think he'll be all right, Ross? Perhaps you hit him too hard.'

Ross made a scowling sound. 'He's lucky I didn't break his damned neck!'

'Why? He was only telling the truth.'

He flashed her a dry look. 'You do have a poor opinion of men at the moment, don't you? Look, if it was just casual sex I was after, I could have my pick of a hundred willing females here tonight. I certainly wouldn't attempt to seduce a sophisticated city broad who probably knows more counter-moves than a chess champion. Here, you pat his cheek while I get him a glass of water. But don't bat those long eyelashes at him if he comes round,' he added sarcastically over his shoulder as he strode off. 'He might get the idea you fancy him!'

She squirmed inside, a guilty blush warming her cheeks. But she busied herself doing as he'd asked, trying to awaken the slumped body in the chair. Tapping cheeks didn't work so she started rubbing hands. His head jerked back and two bloodshot blue eyes fluttered open just as Ross returned with a couple of glasses in his hands.

'Wha—what hit me?' his brother groaned, then clutched at his chin.

'What in hell do you think?' Ross snapped. 'Here, drink this water and sober up a bit.' He turned to face Vivien. 'This is for you,' he said, and pressed a fluted plastic glass of champagne into her hands. 'Your reward for helping me with lunkhead, here. I didn't think water would be your style.'

'Oh, but I…no, really, I…' She tried to give him back the glass, which brought a scoff of disbelief from his lips. 'Good God, what do you think this is, a ploy to get you drunk so that I can have my wicked way with you? Hell, honey, you have got tickets on yourself.'

Vivien stiffened with instant pique. She lifted the champagne and downed it all in one swallow, rebelliously enjoying every bubbly drop, at the same time reminding herself ruefully not to touch another single mouthful that night. She plonked the empty glass down on the littered table near by and looked Ross straight in the eye. 'Even if I were plastered,' she stated boldly, 'I wouldn't let you touch me!'

The young man sprawled in the plastic chair gave a guffaw of laughter. 'Geez, looks like the legendary Ross Everton must have lost his touch! Isn't she falling down on her knees, begging for your body, like every girl you give the eye to?'

Ross swung on his brother as though he was about to hit him again. 'Gavin, I'm *warning* you!'

'Warning me about what, big brother? What more could you possibly do to me? You've got it all now, everything I've ever wanted.' He struggled to his feet and managed to put a determined look on to his weakly handsome face. 'Let me warn *you*, brother, dear,' he blustered. 'Watch your back, because one day it's going to be *me* taking something that's *yours*! You mark my words.' And he lurched off back into the marquee, colliding with several people on the way.

'Will he be all right?' Vivien asked, worried.

'Tonight, you mean? I hope so. God knows why he has to get so damned drunk on these occasions. When he drinks to excess, he goes crazy.'

He's not the only one, Vivien thought, eyeing the empty champagne glass with a degree of concern. *I* don't even need to go to excess. My troubles start around glass number three.

She looked back at Ross, who was rubbing his temple with an agitated forefinger. She forgot about being annoyed with his earlier remarks, seeing only a human being weighed down with problems. And her heart went out to him.

But along with the sympathy she felt a certain amount of curiosity. Was his brother being sarcastic when he'd referred to him as legendary? And legendary in what way, for goodness' sake? His sexual prowess? Vivien's gaze skated over Ross's macho build. He was certainly virile-looking enough to be a womaniser.

There were other questions too teasing at her female curiosity. 'What did Gavin mean,' she asked in the end, 'when he said you've got everything he ever wanted?'

Ross shrugged. 'Who knows? The management of the property, maybe. Or Dad's good opinion. He thinks Gavin's an irresponsible fool. Though Gavin can only blame himself if Dad thinks that. He keeps acting like one. Last year, at this ball, he drove the utility into the creek and nearly drowned. You'd think by twenty-five he'd have started to grow up.'

'Twenty-*five*? He doesn't seem that old.'

'He *looks* his age. He just doesn't act it.'

'Is that why you came along tonight? To see he didn't do it again?'

He nodded. 'I don't think Dad needs any more stress right now.'

Vivien was impressed with his warm concern for his father. 'And your mother?' she queried. 'How's she coping with your father's stroke?' One of Vivien's uncles had had a stroke a couple of years previously and her aunt had almost had a nervous breakdown coping with his agonisingly slow recuperation.

'Mum's dead,' came the brusque reply. 'There's just Dad, Gavin and me.'

'Oh…'

'Yes, I know,' he muttered, and frowned in the direction of the marquee. 'You're sorry and I'm sorry. More than you'll ever know.' His head snapped back to give her a long, thoughtful look.

She squirmed under his intense gaze, especially when his eyes dropped to inspect her considerable cleavage, which the bolero wasn't designed to hide.

'Well,' he sighed at last, eyes lifting back to her face, 'I'd better go and check up on Gavin before he picks a fight with someone else, someone who won't know to pull his punches. Goodbye, Vivien Roberts. Time for you to go back to your world and me to mine.'

He went to move away, but couldn't seem to drag his eyes from her. 'Hell, but you're one beautiful woman. A man would have to be mad to get mixed up with you anyway. Still, I'd like to have a little more to remember than a mere dance!'

Before she realised what he had in mind, he pulled her into his arms and kissed her, his mouth grinding down on hers, his teeth hard. Only for the briefest second did his lips force hers apart, his tongue plunging forward with a single impassioned thrust before he tore his mouth away. Without looking at her again, he spun round and strode off, back into the marquee.

She stared after him, the back of her hand against her mouth. She wasn't at all aware of Irving coming to stand beside her, not till he spoke.

'Hey, Viv, what was that all about? Who *was* that guy?'

Vivien blinked and turned to focus dazedly on her colleague. 'What did you say, Irving?'

He frowned at her. 'Get with it, Viv. It's not like you to go round kissing strange blokes then looking as if you're on cloud nine. Aren't you supposed to be living with some chap back in Sydney? You're not getting swept up with the atmosphere of this Roman orgy, are you?'

She gathered herself with a bitter laugh. 'Not likely. And I'm not living with anyone any more, Irving. He tossed me over for someone else.'

Irving looked surprised. 'What is he, a flaming idiot?'

Vivien's smile was wry. 'That's sweet of you, Irving. But no, Earl's not an idiot. He's a banker.'

Since Irving didn't socialise at the channel, he had never actually met Earl. Vivien only knew as much about Irving as she did because they had worked together before and he was quite a chatterer on the job.

Irving chuckled. 'Well, a banker's not much different from an idiot, judging by the state of the economy. You're probably well rid of him. But that doesn't mean you should encourage any of the males here tonight, sweetheart. They're all tanked up and ready to fly, yet most of them don't have a flight plan. It's gung-ho and away they go! You should see them out behind the marquee.' He rolled his eyes expressively. 'No. Come to think of it, *don't* go and see. Not unless you want to research a programme on the more adventurous positions from the *Kama Sutra*!'

Vivien was astonished. 'That bad, is it? I thought everything was fairly low-key, by city standards.'

'Gracious, girl! Where have you been this last half-hour? Things are really hotting up around here.'

'*Really*?' She wasn't sure whether to believe him or not. Irving's sense of humour included exaggeration.

He nodded sagely. 'Really. The only safe place now is *inside* the marquee, but, judging by the exodus to the nether regions down by the infamous creek, that'll be empty soon except for the band. Which reminds me—you haven't interviewed them yet. Maybe you could do that during their next break.'

'Good idea.'

Vivien, re-entering the marquee, doubted that it would empty as Irving predicted, for there was still a huge crowd of fans standing around the band, clapping and singing, as well as dozens of couples dancing. She and Irving took up positions behind the bandstand to wait for the music to stop.

It didn't seem in a hurry to, one number following another. Vivien spotted Ross's tall head once, very briefly, and the sighting agitated her. She didn't want to think about him any more. She certainly didn't want to think about that disturbing kiss. It had sent sensations down to her toes that not even the longest, most sensuous kiss of Earl's could do, which was all very confusing.

Don't think about either of them, she kept telling herself. It's crazy. Futile. *Stupid*!

But to no avail. She couldn't seem to stop. She especially couldn't get her mind off Ross. He intrigued her, whether she wanted him to or not!

'Another glass of champagne?' a low male voice suddenly whispered in her ear.

She jumped and spun round, knocking an arm in the process and spilling some of the champagne Ross was holding.

'Oh, dear, I'm so sorry!' she gasped.

'So am I,' he said, and smiled with apologetic sincerity at her. 'I shouldn't have kissed you like that. Forgive me?'

She looked up into his quite beautiful blue eyes and felt a real churning in her stomach. It threw her into even more confusion.

'Oh, for Pete's sake, forgive him,' Irving drawled from beside her. 'And give me that damned mike. This band looks as if it's going to keep playing till the year 2000. I think I'll go off and take some sneaky bits down at the creek, all by myself. You go and do some flying, Viv. You deserve it if you've been banking all this time.'

'What did he mean by that?' Ross asked once he'd moved off.

'A private joke,' Vivien said, and struggled to smother a mad chuckle. Not since Earl's ghastly phone call had she felt like laughing about their breakup. And in truth, her perverse humour didn't last for long. Thinking about Earl only served to remind her that what she was feeling for Ross couldn't be real. It was an aberration. A cruel joke of nature.

'Have I said something wrong, Vivien? You look... distressed, all of a sudden.'

She gazed searchingly up into his handsome face, clinging to the various differences from Earl. But his features began to blur together and it was a few seconds before she realised tears had swum into her eyes.

'Here, drink this,' Ross urged, and pressed the plastic glass into her hands. 'It'll make you feel better.'

She hesitated, blinking madly till she had control of herself, all the while staring down into the glass, which was about three-quarters full. Perhaps it *would* make her feel better. Less uptight. Less wretched. There was no real danger. This drink wouldn't even bring her up to her two-glass limit.

'To absent bastards,' she toasted, holding the glass up briefly before quaffing the champagne down. 'Now, where's the fireplace?' she said, putting a forced smile on her face.

'*Fireplace*?'

'To smash the glass into. Oh, I can't,' she sighed, examining the glass in mock disappointment. 'It's plastic.'

She looked up and flashed Ross what she thought was her most winning smile. Little did she know how brittle it looked, and how heartbreakingly vulnerable were her eyes.

'So is your Earl,' he murmured, 'if he let a girl like you get away.'

Vivien's whole throat contracted as an instant lump claimed it. 'I...I wish you wouldn't say things like that.'

'Why? Don't you believe me?' he asked gently.

'Does anyone believe in their own worth after rejection?'

'I should hope so.'

She gave him a bitter look. 'Then you haven't ever been rejected, Ross Everton. Perhaps if you had, you'd know how I feel. And how your brother feels.'

Vivien saw she had struck a nerve with her statement, and regretted it immediately. Ross might not be a saint, but she couldn't see him deliberately hurting his younger brother. Gavin was indeed a fool, trying to blame someone else for the consequences of his own stupid and irresponsible behaviour.

Before she could formulate an apology, Ross spoke.

'Gavin's passed out in the back of his station wagon. From past experience, he'll sleep till morning. Which leaves me free to enjoy the rest of the evening. I thought that perhaps you might...' He hesitated, his eyes searching hers as though trying to gauge her reaction in advance.

'Might what?' she probed, heart fluttering.

'Go for a walk with me.'

'W—where?' she asked, feeling a jab of real alarm. Not so much at his invitation, but at the funny tingling feeling that was spreading over her skin. And now she detected a slight muzziness in her head.

She frowned down at the empty glass in her hands. Perhaps the champagne had been a particularly potent brew... Or maybe on her empty stomach the alcohol had gone to her head, almost as if it had been shot straight into her veins.

Ross shrugged. 'Not many places to go. Down towards the creek, I suppose. It's a couple of hundred yards beyond the back of the marquee.'

'Irving said I wasn't to go down there,' she said with a dry laugh, though inwardly frowning at how hot she felt all of a sudden. Her palms were clammy, too.

There was no doubt about it. The alcohol had hit her system hard. A walk in some fresh air would probably be the quickest way to sober her up, but she wasn't ignorant of the dangers such a walk presented.

She lifted firm eyes. 'Just a walk, Ross?'

He settled equally firm eyes back on her. 'I'm not about to make promises I won't keep. You're a very lovely and desirable woman, Vivien. I'm likely to try kissing you again, and I won't be in such a hurry this time.'

His eyes dropped to her mouth and she gasped, stunned by the shock of desire that charged through her.

Don't go with him, common sense warned.

Before she could open her mouth to decline he took her free hand quite forcibly and started pulling her behind the bandstand. 'There's a flap in the tent we can squeeze through back here,' he urged. 'We'll go through the car park and down to the creek, but well away from the other carousers.'

Vivien quickly found herself outside, any further argument dying on her lips when the fresh air hit her flushed face. She breathed in deeply, sighing with relief as her head started to clear. 'Oh, that *is* better.'

'I was certainly getting stuffy in there,' Ross agreed. 'It's a warm night.'

'Is it ever anything else but warm in this neck of the woods?' She laughed.

'Too right it is. Some nights it's positively freezing. Come on. It'll be very pleasant down by the creek.' He took her hand again, which brought a sharp look from Vivien.

He smiled at her warning glare and quite deliberately lifted her hand to his mouth, kissing each fingertip before turning her hand over and pressing her palm to his mouth. Her eyes widened when his lips opened and she felt his tongue start tracing erotic circles over her skin.

One small part of her brain kept telling her to yank her hand away. The rest was dazed into compliance with the sheer sensual pleasure of it all.

'You…you shouldn't be doing that,' she husked at last.

He lifted his mouth away, but kept her hand firmly in his grasp. 'Why?' Dragging her to him, he dropped her hand to cup her face, all the while staring down into her startled brown eyes. 'You're a free agent, aren't you? Why shouldn't I kiss you? Why shouldn't you kiss me?'

'Because…'

His mouth was coming closer to hers and her heart was going mad.

'Because—' she tried again.

'Because nothing,' he growled, and claimed her parted lips, his arms sweeping round her back in an embrace as confining as a strait-jacket.

When he released her a couple of minutes later, Vivien was in a state of shock. When he put his arm around her shoulder and started leading her through the car park in the direction of the creek, she was still not capable of speech.

Had Earl been able to arouse her so completely and totally with just a kiss? she was thinking dazedly. She didn't think so. When he'd made love to her, most of the time her desire had just been reaching a suitable pitch as he was finishing. Yet here...tonight...with Ross...

Perhaps she *was* tipsier than she realised. Alcohol did have a way of blasting her inhibitions to pieces.

'Are you always this silent when a man kisses you?' Ross murmured into her ear. He stopped then and turned to press her up against one of the parked cars, taking her mouth once more in another devastating kiss. She was struggling for air by the time he let her go, her heart going at fifty to the dozen. She was also blisteringly aware of Ross's arousal pressing against her. With great difficulty she ignored the excitement his desire inflamed in her, concentrating instead on the implication of what she was doing.

Truly, she could not let this continue. It wasn't fair to him. And, quite frankly, not to herself. She had never felt such desire, such excitement. In a minute or two, she wouldn't be able to stop even if she wanted to.

'Ross,' she said shakily as she tried to push him away, 'we have to stop this. We're both getting...excited, and I...I don't go in for one-night stands.'

'Neither do I,' he grated, stubbornly refusing to let her go.

'Ross, try to be sensible,' she argued, her stomach fluttering wildly. 'You're country. I'm city. After tonight we won't ever see each other again. I'm very attracted to you, but...' She shook her head, and carefully omitted to add anything about his physical resemblance to her ex-lover.

'Those problems are not insurmountable,' he said. 'Vivien, this doesn't have to stop at tonight. I often come down to Sydney to visit Dad in hospital and—'

She placed three fingers across his mouth and shook her head again, her eyes truly regretful. 'No, Ross. It won't work. Believe me when I tell you that. And please,' she groaned when he took her hand and started kissing it again, 'don't keep trying to seduce me. I...I'm only human and you're a very sexy man. But I don't really want you.'

He stopped kissing her palm then, lifting his head to peer down at her with thoughtful eyes. 'I don't think you know what you want, Vivien,' he said tautly.

'I know I don't want to act cheaply,' she countered, cheeks flaming under his reproving gaze.

His smile was odd as he dropped her hand. 'A woman like you would never be cheap.'

'Are you being sarcastic?' she flared.

He seemed genuinely taken aback. 'Not at all.'

'Oh...I thought—'

'You think too much,' he said softly, laying such a gentle hand against her cheek that she almost burst into tears.

She swallowed the lump in her throat and lifted a proud chin. 'Better to think tonight than to wake up pregnant in the morning.'

His surprised, 'You're not on the Pill?' brought an instant flush. For of course she was. Earl had adamantly

refused to take responsibility for contraception right from
the start of their affair, claiming it was in *her* interests
that she took charge of such matters. *She* would be the
one left with an unwanted baby. Vivien could see now
that it was just another example of Earl's selfishness.

'Actually, yes, I am,' she admitted. 'But there are *other*
concerns besides pregnancy these days.'

'Not with me there aren't,' he bit out.

She viewed this statement with some cynicism. 'Really?' Her eyes flicked over his very male and very attractive body. 'I wouldn't have taken you for the celibate
type, Ross.' His brother had implied just the opposite,
Vivien remembered ruefully.

'One doesn't have to be celibate to be careful.'

'And would you have been careful tonight if I'd given
you the go-ahead?' she challenged.

A slash of red burnt a guilty path across his cheeks.
'This was different,' he muttered, and lifted both hands to
rake agitatedly through his hair.

Her laugh was scornful. 'I don't see how.'

His blue eyes glittered dangerously as they swung back
to her. 'Then you're a fool, Vivien Roberts. A damned
fool!'

For a second, she thought he was going to grab her and
kiss her again. But he didn't. Instead, his mouth creased
back into the strangest smile. It was both bitter and self-
mocking. 'Look, let's walk, shall we? That's what you
obviously came out here for. And don't worry your pretty
little head. I won't lay a single finger on you unless I get
a gold-edged invitation.'

He set off at a solid pace through the rows of cars,
Vivien trailing disconsolately behind him. For she knew

in the deepest dungeons of her mind, in the place reserved for unmentionable truths, that she didn't want Ross to lay a *single* finger on her. She wanted *all* his fingers, and *both* his hands. She wanted every wonderfully virile part of him.

CHAPTER FOUR

'CAN you slow down a bit?' she complained when the distance between them became ridiculous.

Ross had long left the car park and was almost at the tree-lined creek, while she was still halfway across the intervening paddock. If she'd tried to keep up with him she'd probably have fallen down one of the rabbit holes hidden in the grass. She'd already tripped a few times over rocks and logs and the like. Lord knew what her high heels looked like by now.

He stopped abruptly and threw a black look over his shoulder. Moonlight slanted across the angles of his face and she caught her breath as, for the first time, she saw little resemblance to Earl. His features suddenly looked leaner, harder, stronger. Yet they still did the most disturbing things to her stomach.

She slowed to a crawl as she approached, her eyes searching the ice-blue of his, trying to make sense of what she kept feeling for this man, even now, when he no longer reminded her so much of Earl. She couldn't even cling to the belief that she was tipsy, for the brisk walk had totally cleared her head.

His eyes changed as she stared up at him, at first to bewilderment, then to a wary watchfulness, and finally to one of intuitive speculation. They narrowed as they raked over her, his scrutiny becoming explicitly sexual as it lingered on specific areas of her body.

A wave of sheer sensual weakness washed through Vivien and she swayed towards him. 'Ross, I...I—'

He didn't wait for the gilt-edged invitation. He simply read her body language and scooped her hard against him, kissing her till she was totally breathless. 'God, I want you,' he rasped against her softly swollen mouth. 'I'll go mad if I don't have you. Don't say no...'

She said absolutely nothing as he lifted her up into his arms, carrying her with huge strides to the creek bank, where he lowered her on to the soft grass under a weeping willow. But her eyes were wide, her mind in chaos, her heart beating frantically in her chest.

'I won't ever hurt you, Vivien,' he whispered soothingly, and lay down beside her, bending over to kiss her, softly now, almost reverently.

Dimly she heard the sounds of distant revellers, their shouting and laughter. But even that receded as Ross's hand found her breast.

'You're so beautiful,' he muttered, and, pushing back the taffeta, he bent his mouth to the hardened peak.

Vivien closed her eyes and held his head at her breast, trying to take in the intensity of feeling that was welling up inside her. Briefly she remembered all that had happened to her over the last few days, and for a second she felt overwhelmed with guilt. She wasn't in love with Ross, couldn't possibly be. No more than he could be in love with her.

A tortured whimper broke from her lips.

'What's the matter, sweetheart?' Ross said gently, and returned to sip at her mouth. 'Tell me...'

'Oh, Ross,' she cried, her eyes fluttering open, raw pain in their depths. But as they gazed into his brilliant blue eyes, which were glittering above her with the most incredible passion in their depths, the most seductive yearning, she melted. He wanted her. He *really* wanted her. Not like Earl. Earl had never *really* wanted her.

An obsession. That's what he'd called his feelings for her. An obsession... An unhealthy, an unwated need, one to be fought against, to be got over like something nasty and repulsive.

What she saw in Ross's eyes wasn't anything like that. It was normal and natural and quite beautiful.

She trembled as she clasped him close. 'Say that you love me,' she whispered. 'That's all I ask.'

He lifted his head to stare down at her, blue eyes startled.

'Oh, you don't have to mean it,' she cried, and clung to him. 'Just say it!'

A darkly troubled frown gathered on his brow and for a long, long moment he just looked at her. But then his hands came up to cradle her face and he gazed at her with such tenderness that she felt totally shattered. 'I love you, Vivien. I really, truly love you...'

She shuddered her despair at demanding such a pretence, but could no more deny the need to hear them than the need Ross was evoking within her woman's body.

'Show me,' she groaned. 'Make me forget everything but here...and now...'

At the first slightly vague moments of consciousness, Vivien was aware of nothing but a very fuzzy head and a throat as dry as the Simpson Desert. Her eyes blinked open to glance around her hotel room, and straight away she remembered.

With chest immediately constricted, she rolled over and stared at Ross beside her, flat on his back, sound asleep, his naked chest rising and falling in the deep and even breathing of the exhausted.

Rounded eyes went from him to the floor beside the bed, where her beautiful taffeta dress was lying in a sodden heap. Her black lace panties were still hanging from the arm-rest of the chair in the corner where Ross had carelessly tossed them. Her bolero and shoes, she recalled, were still down beside the creek.

Oh, my God, she moaned silently, the night before rushing back in Technicolor. How could I have behaved so...so outrageously? To have let Ross make love to me on the river-bank was bad enough. But what about later?

Her face flamed as guilt and shame consumed her.

She should never have allowed him to talk her into going skinny-dipping in the moonlit creek afterwards. Naked, he was even more insidiously attractive than he'd been in his dashing dinner suit, his body all brown and lean and hard.

Vivien had been fascinated by the feel of his well-honed muscles. She'd touched him innocently enough at first, holding on to his shoulders to stop herself from tiring as she trod water in the deep. But her hands hadn't stayed on his shoulders for long. They had begun to wander. Once she had started exploring his body, one thing had quickly led to another and, before she knew it, Ross was urging her into the shallows, where he'd taken her again right then and there in the water.

Afterwards, he had carried her limp body back on to the bank where he'd dressed her as best he could, then carried her back to the hotel. Vivien could still remember the look on the hotel proprietor's face when Ross had carried her past his desk and up the stairs.

By this time her conscience had begun to raise its damning head, but Ross managed to ram it back down with more drugging kisses in her room, more knowing caresses. Before she knew it, he was undressing her again and urging her to further amazing new heights of sensuality.

Vivien blushed furiously to think of her abandoned response to his lovemaking.

I have to get out of here. Fast. I couldn't possibly face him. I'd die! God, I even made him say he *loved* me!

She cringed in horror, then even more so as she recalled how after the last time here on the bed she'd actually wept. With the sheer intensity of her pleasure, not distress. Ross's lovemaking had seemed to possess not just her body but her very soul, taking her to a level of emotional and physical satisfaction she had never known before.

At least…that was how it had *seemed* at the time…

Looking back now, Vivien realised it couldn't *possibly* have been as marvellous an experience as she kept imagining. Certainly not in any emotional sense. Ross was simply a very skilled lover, knowing just what buttons to push, what words to say to make a woman melt. After all, she'd only asked him to say he loved her once, but he'd told her over and over. There were times when a more naïve woman might have believed he really *did* love her— he sounded and looked so sincere!

She darted a quick glance over at his face, at his softly parted lips. And shuddered. There wasn't a single inch of her flesh that those lips hadn't passed over at some time during the night.

Once again, she felt heat invade her face. Not to mention other parts of her body.

Thank God the bathroom is down the hall, Vivien thought shakily. I'll get my things together and slip out of this room and be gone before he opens a single one of those incredible blue eyes of his. For if I wait, I'm not sure what might happen...

A few minutes later she was knocking on Irving's door. He looked decidedly bleary as he opened it wearing nothing but striped boxer shorts.

'Viv?' He yawned. 'What are you doing up? I thought you'd be out of it for hours.' He gave her a slow, sly grin. 'Bert informed me that you were escorted back to your room at some ungodly hour by someone he called the "legendary Ross Everton". I presume he was the handsome hunk you were with earlier in the night. Did he—er—cure you of the banker?'

Vivien coloured fiercely, though her whirling mind was puzzling again over that word 'legendary'. Legendary in what way? Her colour increased when she realised it probably meant Ross's reputation with women. No doubt she had just spent the night with a very well-known local stud. Why, even his own brother had suggested Ross was a real ladies' man, with an infallible success rate.

Squashing down a mad mixture of dismay and mortification, Vivien gave Irving one of her most quelling 'shut-up-and-listen' looks. 'I need to be out of here five minutes ago, Irving. Do you think you can get a rustle on?'

'What's the emergency?'

'Shall we just say I don't want to see a certain "legendary" person when he finally wakes up?'

Irving pursed his lips and nodded slowly. 'Mornings after can be a tad sticky.'

'I would have used another word, like *humiliating*! You and I know this is not like me at all, Irving. I'm quietly appalled at myself.'

'You're only human, love. Don't be too hard on yourself. We all let our hair down occasionally.'

'Yes, well, I'd appreciate it if this particular hair-letting-down didn't get around the channel. Not all my colleagues are as good a friend as you, Irving.'

'Mum's the word.'

'Thanks. Look, I'll fix up the hotel bill and meet you at the car as soon as possible.'

'I'll be there before you are.'

Irving dropped Vivien outside her block of flats at seven that evening. She carried her overnight bag wearily up the two flights of stairs, where she inserted the key into the door numbered nine. She pushed the door open and walked in, switching on the light and kicking the door shut behind her in one movement.

Her mouth gaped open as she looked around the living-room in stunned disbelief. Because it was empty!

Well, not exactly empty. The phone was sitting on the carpet against the far wall, and three drooping pot plants huddled in a corner. Gone were the lounge and dining suites, the cocktail cabinet, the coffee-table, the television, the sound system and the oak sideboard, along with everything that had been on or in them. The walls were bare too, pale rectangles showing where various paintings had been hanging.

Vivien dropped the overnight bag at her feet and

walked numbly into the kitchen. A dazed search revealed that she was still the proud owner of some odd pieces of chipped crockery and some assorted cutlery. The toaster was the only appliance still in residence, probably because it had been a second-hand one, given to them by her mother. The fridge was there too. But it had come with the flat. Vivien approached the two bedrooms with a growing sense of despair.

The main bedroom was starkly empty, except for her side of the built-in wardrobes. The guest bedroom shocked her in reverse, because it actually contained a single bed complete with linen.

'Oh, thanks a lot, Earl,' she muttered before slumping down on the side of the bed and dissolving into tears.

Five minutes later she was striding back into the living-room and angrily snatching the phone up from the floor. But then she hesitated, and finally dropped the receiver back down into its cradle.

There was no point in ringing Earl. Absolutely no point. For she hadn't paid for a single one of the items he'd taken from their flat. When she'd moved in, Earl, the financial wizard, had suggested *she* pay for the food each week while *he* paid for any other goods they needed. Over the eighteen months he'd bought quite a bit, but she'd also forked out a lot of cash on entertaining Earl's business acquaintances. He always liked the best in food and wine.

Now she wondered with increasing bitterness if he'd known all along how their affair would end and had arranged things so that he'd finish up with all the material possessions she'd assumed they co-owned.

A fair-minded person would have split everything fifty-

fifty. To do what Earl had done was not only cruel. It also underlined that all he'd thrown at her over the telephone was true. He had never loved her. He'd simply used her. She'd been his housekeeper and his whore! And he'd got them both cheap!

But then she *was* cheap, wasn't she? she berated herself savagely. Only cheap women went to bed with a man within an hour or two of meeting him, without any real thought of his feelings, without caring where it led, without...

'Oh, my God!' she gasped aloud, and, with the adrenalin of a sudden shock shooting through her body, Vivien raced over to where she had dropped her bag. She reefed open the zip. But her fumbling fingers couldn't find what she was looking for. Yet they had to be here. They *had* to!

A frantic glance at her watch told her it was almost eight, thirteen hours after she usually took her pill. In the end she tipped the whole contents of the bag out on to the floor and they were were!

Snaffling them up, she pressed Sunday's pill through the foil and swallowed it. But all the while her doctor's warnings went round and round in her mind.

'This is a very low-dosage pill, Vivien, and *must* be taken within the same hourly span each day. To deviate by too long could be disastrous.'

The enormity of this particular disaster did not escape Vivien. She sank down into a sitting position on the carpet and hugged herself around the knees, rocking backwards and forwards in pained distress. 'Oh, no,' she wailed. 'Please, God...not that...I couldn't bear it...'

Vivien might have given herself up to total despair at

that moment if the phone hadn't rung just then, forcing her to pull herself together.

'Yes?' she answered, emotion making her voice tight and angry. If it was Earl ringing he was going to be very, very sorry he had.

'Vivien? Is there something wrong?'

Vivien closed her eyes tight. Her mother... Her loving but very intuitive mother.

She gathered every resource she had. 'No, Mum. Everything's fine.'

'Are you sure?'

'Yes. Positive.' Smiles in her voice.

'I hope so.' Wariness in her mother's.

'What were you ringing up about, Mum?'

Vivien's mother was never one to ring for idle gossip. There was always a specific reason behind the call.

'Well, next Sunday week's your father's birthday, as you know, and I was planning a family dinner for him, and I was hoping you would come this time, now that Earl's in Melbourne. That man never seems to like you going to family gatherings,' her soft-hearted mother finished as accusingly as she could manage.

'Of course I'll be there,' she reassured, ignoring the gibe about Earl. Not that it wasn't true, come to think of it. Earl had never wanted to share her with her family.

She sighed. Perhaps in a fortnight's time she'd feel up to telling her mother about their breakup. Though, of course, in a fortnight's time she'd probably also be on the verge of a nervous breakdown, worrying if she was pregnant or not. God, what was to become of her?

'Do you want me to bring anything beside a present?' she asked. 'Some wine, maybe?'

'Only your sweet self, darling.'

The 'darling' almost did it. Tears swam into Vivien's eyes and her chin began to quiver. 'Oh, goodness, there's someone at the door, Mum. Must go. See you Sunday week about noon, OK?'

She just managed to hang up before she collapsed into a screaming heap on the floor, crying her eyes out.

CHAPTER FIVE

'I'M SORRY, Viv,' Mervyn said without any real apology in his voice. 'But that's the way it is. *Across Australia* has received another cut in budget and I have to trim staff. I've decided to do it on a last-on, first-to-go basis.'

'I see,' was Vivien's controlled reply. She knew there was no point in mentioning that fan mail suggested she was one of the show's most popular reporters. Mervyn was a man's man. He also never went back on a decision, once he'd made it.

'There's nothing else going at the channel?' she asked, trying to maintain a civil politeness in the face of her bitter disappointment. 'No empty slots anywhere?'

'I'm sorry, Viv,' he said once more. 'But you know how things are…'

What could she possibly say? If the quality of her work had not swayed him then no other argument would. Besides, she had too much pride to beg.

'Personnel has already made up your cheque,' he went on matter-of-factly when she remained stubbornly silent. 'You can pick it up at Reception.'

Now Vivien *was* shocked. Shocked and hurt. She propelled herself up from the chair on to shaky legs. 'But I'm supposed to get a month's notice,' she argued. 'My contract states that—'

'Your contract also states,' Mervyn overrode curtly, 'that you can receive a month's extra pay in lieu of notice.

That's what we've decided to do in your case. For security reasons,' he finished brusquely.

She sucked in a startled breath. 'What on earth does that mean? What security reasons?'

'Come, now, Viv, it wouldn't be the first time that a disgruntled employee worked out their time here, all the while relaying our ideas to our opposition.'

'But…but you *know* I wouldn't do any such thing!'

His shrug was indifferent, his eyes hard and uncompromising. 'I don't make the policies around here, Viv. I only enforce them. If I hear of anything going I'll let you know.' With that, he extended a cold hand.

Vivien took it limply, turning on stunned legs before walking shakily from the room. This isn't happening to me, she told herself over and over. I'm in some sort of horrible nightmare.

In the space of a few short days, she had lost Earl, and now her job…

'Viv?' the receptionist asked after she'd been standing in front of the desk staring into space for quite some time. 'Are you all right?'

Vivien composed herself with great difficulty, covering her inner turmoil with a bland smile. 'Just wool-gathering. I was told there would be a letter for me here…'

Vivien walked around the flat in a daze. She still couldn't believe what had happened back at the channel. When she'd arrived at work that morning, she'd thought Mervyn had wanted to talk to her to see how the segment at Wallaby Creek had gone over the weekend. Instead, she'd been summarily retrenched.

How ironic, she thought with rising bitterness. She had

virtually lost Earl because of that job. And now…the job was no more.

Tears threatened. But she blinked them away. She was fed up with crying, and totally fed up with life! What had she ever done to deserve to be dumped like that—first by the man she loved, then by an employer to whom she had given nothing but her best? It was unfair and unjust and downright unAustralian!

Well, I'll just have to get another job, she realised with a resurgence of spirit. A *better* job!

Such as what? the voice of grim logic piped up. All the channels are laying off people right, left and centre. Unemployment's at a record high.

'I'll find something,' she determined out loud, and marched into the kitchen, where she put on the kettle to make herself some coffee.

And what if you're pregnant? another little voice inserted quietly.

Vivien's stomach tightened.

'I can't be,' she whispered despairingly. 'That would be too much. Simply too much. Dear God, please don't do that to me as well. *Please*…'

Vivien was just reaching for a cup and saucer when the front doorbell rang. Frowning, she clattered the crockery on to the kitchen counter and glanced at her watch. 'Now who on earth could that be at four fifty-three on a Monday afternoon?' she muttered.

The bell ran again. Quite insistently.

'All right, all right, I'm coming!'

Vivien felt a vague disquiet as she went to open the door. Most of her acquaintances and friends would still be at work. Who could it possibly be?

'Ross!' she gasped aloud at first sight of him, her heart leaping with...what?

He stood there, dressed in blue jeans and a white T-shirt, a plastic carrier-bag in his left hand and a wry smile on his face.

'Vivien,' he greeted smoothly.

For a few seconds neither of them said anything further. Ross's clear blue eyes lanced her startled face before travelling down then up her figure-fitting pink and black suit. By the time his gaze returned to their point of origin Vivien was aware that her heart was thudding erratically in her chest. A fierce blush was also staining her cheeks.

Embarrassment warred with a surprisingly intense pleasure over his reappearance in her life. My God, he'd actually followed her all this way! Perhaps he didn't look at the other night as a one-night stand after all. Perhaps he really cared about her.

And perhaps not, the bitter voice of experience intervened, stilling the flutterings in her heart.

'What...what are you doing here?' she asked warily.

He shrugged. 'I had to come to Sydney to visit my father and I thought you might like the things you left behind.' He held out the plastic bag.

Her dismay was sharp. So! He hadn't followed her at all. Not really. She wasn't deceived by his excuse for dropping by. The way he'd looked at her just now was not the look of a man who'd only come to return something. Vivien knew the score. Ross was going to be in town anyway and thought he might have another sampling of what she'd given him so easily the other night.

Her disappointment quickly fuelled a very real anger. She snatched the plastic bag without looking inside, tossing it behind the door. She didn't want to see her ruined bolero and shoes, not needing any more reminders of her disgusting behaviour the other night. Ross's presence on her doorstep was reminder enough.

'How kind of you,' she retorted sarcastically. 'But how did you find out my address? It's not in the phone book.'

His eyes searched her face as though trying to make sense of her ill temper. 'Once I explained to the receptionist at the channel about your having left some of your things behind at the Wallaby Creek hotel,' he said, 'and that I had come all this way to return them, she gave me your address.'

'But you didn't come all this way just to return them, did you?' she bit out. 'Look, Ross, if you think you're going to take up where you left off then I suggest you think again. I have no intention of—'

'You're *ashamed* of what we did,' he cut in with surprise in his voice.

Her cheeks flamed. 'What did you *expect*? That I'd be *proud* of myself?'

'I don't see why not... What we shared the other night, Vivien, was something out of the ordinary. You must know how I feel about you. You must also have known I would not let you get away that easily.'

'Oh? And how *does* the legendary Ross Everton feel about little ole me?' she lashed out, annoyed that he would think her so gullible. 'Surely you're not going to declare undying love, are you?' she added scathingly. 'Not Ross Everton, the famous—or is it infamous?—country Casanova!'

His eyes had narrowed at her tirade, their light blue darkening with a black puzzlement. 'I think you've been listening to some twisted tales, Vivien. My legendary status, if one could call it such, has nothing to do with my being a Casanova.'

Now it was her turn to stare with surprise. 'Then what…what?'

He shrugged off her bumbled query, his penetrating gaze never leaving her. 'I *do* care about you, Vivien. Very much. When I woke to find you gone, I was…' His mouth curved back into a rueful smile. 'Let's just say I wasn't too pleased. I thought, damn and blast, that city bitch has just used me. But after I'd had time to think about it I knew that couldn't be so. You're too straightforward, Vivien. Too open. Too sweet…'

He took a step towards her then. Panic-stricken, she backed up into the flat. When Ross followed right on inside, then shut the door, her eyes flung wide.

'Don't be alarmed,' he soothed. 'I told you once and I'll tell you again: I won't ever hurt you. But I refuse to keep discussing our private lives in a damned hallway.' He glanced around the living-room, its emptiness clearly distracting him from what he'd been about to add. 'You're moving out?'

She shook her head. Somehow, words would not come. Her mind was whirling with a lot of mixed-up thoughts. For even if Ross was genuine with his feelings for her, what future could they have together? *Her* feelings for *him* had no foundation. They were nothing but a cruel illusion, sparked by his likeness to Earl.

'Then what happened to your furniture?' Ross asked.

She cleared her throat. 'Earl…Earl took it all.'

'*All* of it?'

Her laugh was choked and dry. 'He left me a single bed. Wasn't that nice of him?'

'Could win him the louse-of-the-year award.'

Vivien saw the pity in Ross's eyes and hated it.

Suddenly, the whole grim reality of her situation rushed in on her like a swamping wave, bringing with it a flood of self-pity. The tears she had kept at bay all day rushed in with a vengeance.

'Oh, God,' she groaned, her hands flying up to cover her crumpling face. 'God,' she repeated, then began to sob.

Despite her weeping, she was all too hotly aware of Ross gathering her into his strong arms, cradling her distraught, disintegrating self close to the hard warmth of his chest.

'Don't cry, darling,' he murmured. 'Please don't cry. He's not worth it, can't you see that? He didn't really love you...or care about you... Don't waste your tears on him... Don't...'

To Vivien's consternation, her self-pitying outburst dried up with astonishing swiftness, replaced by a feeling of sexual longing so intense that it refused to be denied. Hardly daring to examine what she was doing, she felt her arms steal around Ross's waist, her fingers splaying wide as they snaked up his back. With a soft moan of surrender, she nestled her face into his neck, pressing gently fluttering lips to the pulse-point at the base of his throat.

She felt his moment of acute stillness, *agonised* over it. Her body desperately wanted him to seduce her again. But her mind—her *conscience*—implored with her to stop before it was too late.

This is wrong, Vivien, she pleaded with herself. Wrong! You don't love him. What in God's name is the matter with you? Stop it now!

She wrenched out of his arms just as they tightened around her, the action making them both stagger backwards in opposite directions.

'I'm s—sorry,' she blurted out. 'I...I shouldn't have done that. I'm not myself today. I...I just lost my job, and coming so soon after Earl's leaving... Not that that's any excuse...' She lifted her hand to her forehead in a gesture of true bewilderment. 'I'm not even drunk this time,' she groaned, appalled at herself.

Ross stared across at her. 'What do you mean? You weren't drunk the other night. You'd only had a couple of glasses of champagne. Not even full glasses.'

Her sigh was ragged. 'That's enough for me on an empty stomach. I have this almost allergic reaction to alcohol, you see. It sends me crazy, a bit like your brother, only I don't need nearly as much. I'm a cheap drunk, Ross. A *very* cheap drunk,' she finished with deliberate irony.

'I see,' he said slowly.

'I'm sorry, Ross.'

'So am I. Believe me.' He just stood there, staring at her, his eyes troubled. Suddenly, he sighed, and pulled himself up straight and tall. 'Did I hear rightly just now? You've lost your job?'

'Yes, but not to worry. I'll find something else.' She spoke quickly, impatiently. For she just wanted him to go.

'Are you sure?' he persisted. 'Unemployment's high in the television industry, I hear.'

'I have my family. I'll be fine.'

'They live near by?'

'Parramatta. Look, it…it was nice of you to come all this way to see me again, Ross,' she said stiffly, wishing he would take the hint and leave. She had never felt so wretched, and guilty, and confused.

'Nice?' His smile was bitter. 'Oh, it wasn't nice, Vivien. It was a necessity. I simply *had* to see you again before I…' He broke off with a grimace. 'But that's none of your concern now.'

He gave Vivien an oddly ironic look. Once again, she was struck by his *dissimilarity* to Earl. His facial features might have come out of the same mould. But his expressions certainly didn't. His eyes were particularly expressive, ranging from a chilling glitter of reproach to a blaze of white-hot passion.

Vivien stared at him, remembering only too well how he had looked as he'd made love to her, the way his skin had drawn back tight across his cheekbones, his lips parting, his eyes heavy, as though he were drowning in his desire. Immediately, she felt a tightening inside, followed by a dull ache of yearning.

Did he see the desire in her eyes, the hunger?

Yes, he must have. For his expression changed once more, this time to a type of resolve that she found quite frightening. His hands shot out to grip her waist, yanking her hard against him.

'I don't care if you were drunk,' he rasped. 'I don't care if you're still in love with your stupid bloody Earl. All you have to do is keep looking at me like that and it'll be enough.'

His mouth was hard, his kiss savage. But she found herself giving in to it with a sweet surrender that was far more intoxicating than any amount of alcohol could ever be.

The doorbell ringing again made them both jump.

'Are you expecting anyone?' Ross asked thickly, his mouth in her hair, his hands restless on her back and buttocks.

Vivien shook her head.

Their chests rose and fell with ragged breathing as they waited in silence. The bell rang again. And again.

Ross sighed. 'You'd better answer it.' His hands dropped away from her, lifting to run agitatedly through his hair as he stepped back.

Vivien ran her own trembling hands down her skirt before turning to the door, all the while doing her best to school her face into an expression that would not betray her inner turmoil. One kiss, she kept thinking. One miserable kiss and I'm his for the taking...

She was stunned to find Bob standing on the other side of the door, a bottle of wine under his arm, a triumphant and sickeningly sleazy look on his face.

'Hello, Vivien.' He smirked. 'I dropped by to say how sorry I was about the way Mervyn dismissed you today. I thought we might have a drink together, and then, if you like, we could...'

He broke off when his gaze wandered over Vivien's shoulder, his beady eyes opening wide with true surprise when they encountered Ross standing there.

'Oh...oh, hi, there, Earl,' he called out, clearly flustered. 'I thought you were in Melbourne. Well, it's good to know Viv has someone here in her hour of need. I—er—only called round to offer my sympathy and a shoulder to cry on, but I can see she doesn't need it. I...I guess

I'd better be going. Sorry to interrupt. See you around, Viv. Bye, Earl.'

Vivien could feel Ross's frozen stillness behind her as she slowly shut the door and turned. He looked as if someone had just hit him in the stomach with a sledge-hammer.

'Ross,' she began, 'I—'

'I'm not just *like* your ex-lover, am I, Vivien?' he broke in harshly. 'I'm his damned double!'

She closed her eyes against his pained hurt. 'Almost,' she admitted huskily.

'God...'

Vivien remained silent. Perhaps it was for the best, she reasoned wretchedly. At least now he would see that there was no hope of a real relationship between them and he would leave her alone. For God only knew what would happen if he stayed.

But what if you're already pregnant by him? whispered that niggling voice.

Vivien pushed the horrendous thought aside. Surely fate couldn't be that perverse?

'I want you to open your eyes and look at me, Vivien,' Ross stated in a voice like ice.

She did, and his eyes were as flat and hard as eyes could be. She shrank from the cold fury his gaze projected.

'I want you to confirm that the main reason you responded to me the way you did the other night is because I'm the spitting image of your ex-lover. You were fantasising I was this Earl while I was making love to you, is that correct?'

No, was her instant horrified reaction. *No! It wasn't like that*!

And yet... It had to be so. For if it wasn't, then what had it been? Animal lust? The crude using of any body to assuage sexual frustration? Revenge on Earl, maybe?

None of those things felt right. She refused to accept them. Which only left what Ross had concluded. Perhaps the reason she instinctively rejected that explanation was because her memory of that night had been clouded by alcohol. She recalled thinking the next morning that her pleasure in Ross's lovemaking could not have been so extraordinary, could *not* have propelled her into another world where nothing existed but this man, and this man alone.

'I'm waiting, Vivien,' he demanded brusquely.

'Yes,' she finally choked out, though her tortured eyes slid away from his to the floor. 'Yes...'

He dragged in then exhaled a shuddering breath. 'Great,' he muttered. 'Just great. I'll remember that next time my emotions threaten to get in the way of my common sense. Pardon me if I say I hope I never see you again, Vivien Roberts. Still...you've been an experience, one I bitterly suspect I'll never repeat!'

He didn't look back as he left, slamming the door hard behind him.

It wasn't till a minute or two later that Vivien remembered something that challenged both Ross's conclusion and her own. If her responses had really been for Earl, if her memory of that night had been confused by alcohol and her pleasure not as overwhelming as she had thought, then why had she responded with such shattering intensity to Ross's kiss just now? Why?

None of it made sense.

But then, nothing made sense any more to Vivien. Her

whole world had turned upside-down. Once, she had seen her future so very clearly. Now, there was only a bleak black haziness, full of doubts and fears and insecurities. She wanted quite desperately to run home to her mother, to become a child again, with no decisions to make, no responsibilities to embrace.

But she wasn't a child. She was an adult. A grown woman. She had to work things out for herself.

Vivien did the only thing a sensible, grown-up woman could do. She went to bed and cried herself to sleep.

CHAPTER SIX

'WHEN are you going to tell me what's wrong, dear?'

Vivien stiffened, tea-towel in hand, then slanted a sideways glance at her mother. Peggy Roberts had not turned away from where she stood at the kitchen sink, washing up after her husband Lionel's birthday dinner.

Vivien's stomach began to churn. There she'd been, thinking she had done a splendid job of hiding the turmoil in her heart. Why, she had fairly bubbled all through dinner, sheer force of will pushing the dark realities of the past fortnight way, way to the back of her mind.

Now, her mother's intuitive question sent them all rushing forward, stark in their grimness. She didn't know which was the worst: her growing realisation that she was unlikely to land a decent job in Sydney this side of six months, if ever; the crushing loneliness she felt every time she let herself back into her empty flat; or the terrifying prospect that her fear over being pregnant was fast becoming a definite rather than a doubtful possibility.

Her period had been due two days before and it hadn't arrived. Periods were never late when one was on the Pill. Of course, the delay might have been caused by her having forgotten one, but she didn't think so.

Just thinking about actually having a real baby—*Ross's* baby—sent her into a mental spin.

'Vivien,' her mother resumed with warmth and worry in her voice, 'you do know you can tell me anything, don't you? I promise I won't be shocked, or judgemental. But I can't let you leave here today without knowing what it is that has put you on this razor's edge. The others probably haven't noticed, but they don't know you as well as I do. Your gaiety, my dear, was just a fraction brittle over dinner. Besides, you haven't mentioned Earl once today, and that isn't like you. Not like you at all. Have you had a falling-out with him, dear? Is that it?'

Vivien gave a small, hysterical laugh. 'I wouldn't put it like that exactly.'

'Then how would you put it?' her mother asked gently.

Too gently. Her loving concern sent a lump to Vivien's throat, and tears into her eyes. Forcing them back, she dragged in a shuddering breath then burst forth, nerves and emotion sending the words out in a wild tumble of awful but rather muddled confessions.

'Well, Mum, the truth is that a couple of weeks back Earl gave me the ole heave-ho, told me he didn't love me and that he had found someone else. I was very upset, to put it mildly, but that weekend I had to go out to that Bachelors' and Spinsters' Ball for work. You know, the one they showed on TV last week. And while I was there I met this man who, believe it or not, is practically Earl's double, and I...well, I slept with him on some sort of rebound, I suppose. At least, I think that's why I did it...'

She began wringing the tea-towel. 'But I also forgot my pill, you see, and now I think I might be pregnant. Then on the Monday after that weekend I was retrenched at the channel and that same day Ross came to Sydney to see me, hoping to make a go of things between us, but he found out how much he looked like Earl and jumped to all the right conclusions, which I made worse by telling

him I was sloshed at the time I slept with him anyway.
Not that I was, but you know what drink does to me, and
I had had a bit to drink and...and...as you can see, I'm
in a bit of a mess...'

By this time tears were streaming down her face.

To give her mother credit, she didn't look too much
like a stunned mullet. More like a flapping flounder, holding stunned hands out in front of her, while washing-up
water dripped steadily from her frozen fingertips on to the
cork-tiled floor.

But she quickly pulled herself together, wiping her
soapy hands on the tea-towel she dragged out of Vivien's
hands, then leading her distressed daughter quickly away
from potentially prying eyes into the privacy of her old
bedroom.

'Sit,' she said, firmly settling Vivien down on the white
lace quilt before leaning over to extract several tissues
from the box on the dressing-table and pressing them into
her daughter's hands. She sat down on the bed as well,
then waited a few moments while Vivien blew her nose
and stopped weeping.

'Now, Vivien, I'm not going to pretend that I'm not a
little shocked, no matter what I said earlier. But there's
no point in crying over spilt milk, so to speak. Now, I'm
not sure if I got the whole gist of your story. Ross, I
presume, is the name of the man who may or may not be
the father of your child?'

'Oh, he's the father all right,' Vivien blubbered. 'It's
the child who's a maybe or maybe not. It's a bit too soon
to tell.'

Peggy sighed her relief. 'So you don't really know yet.
You might not be pregnant.'

'Yes, I am,' Vivien insisted wildly. 'I know I am.'

'Vivien! You sound as if you *want* to be pregnant by this man, this…this…stranger who looks like Earl.'

Vivien stared at her startled mother, then shook her head in utter bewilderment. 'I don't know what I want any more, Mum. I…I'm so mixed up and miserable and… Please help me. You always know just what to say to make me see things clearly. Tell me I'm not going mad. Tell me it wasn't wicked of me to do what I did. Tell me you and Dad don't mind if I have a baby, that you'll love me anyway. I've been so worried about everything.'

'Oh, my poor, dear child,' Peggy said gently, and enfolded her in her mother's arms. 'You've really been through the mill, haven't you? Of course you're not going mad. And of course you're not wicked. But as parents we *will* be worried about you having a baby all on your own, so if you are pregnant you'll have to come home and live with us so we can look after you. Come to think of it, you're coming home anyway. You must be horribly lonely in that flat all on your own.'

'You can say that again,' Vivien sniffled.

'You must be horribly lonely in that flat all on your own…'

Vivien pulled back, her eyes snapping up to her mother's. Peggy was smiling. 'Mum! This isn't funny, you know.'

'I know, but I can't help feeling glad that you're not going to marry that horrible Earl.'

'You never said you thought he was horrible before.'

'Yes, well, your father and I didn't want to make him seem any more attractive than you obviously already found him. But believe me, love, I didn't like him at all.

He was the most selfish man I have ever met. Selfish and snobbish. He would have made a dreadful father, too. Simply dreadful. He had no sense of family.'

Vivien nodded slowly in agreement. 'You're right. I can see that now. I can see a lot of things about Earl that I couldn't see before. I don't know why I loved him as much as I did.'

'Well, he could be charming when he chose,' her mother admitted. 'And he was very handsome. Which makes me think that maybe you never loved him. Not really.'

Vivien blinked.

'Maybe it was only a sexual attraction,' Peggy suggested.

Vivien frowned.

'This man you slept with, the one you said looks a lot like Earl—'

'More than a lot,' Vivien muttered.

'Obviously you're one of those women who's always attracted to the same physical type. For some of us it's blond hair and blue eyes, or broad shoulders and a cute butt, or—'

'Mum!' Vivien broke in, shock in her voice.

Peggy smiled at her daughter. 'Do you think you're the only female in this family who's ever been bowled over by a sexual attraction?'

'Well, I...I—'

'Your father wasn't my first man, you know.'

'*Mum!*'

'Will you stop saying "Mum!" like that? It's unnerving. I don't mean I was promiscuous, but there was this other fellow first. I think if I tell you about him you might see that what happened between you and this Ross person was hardly surprising, or wicked.'

'Well, all right…if you say so…'

Peggy drew in a deep breath, then launched into her astonishing tale. At least, Vivien found it astonishing.

'I was eighteen at the time, working as a receptionist with a firm of solicitors while I went to secretarial school at night. Damian was one of the junior partners. Oh, he was a handsome devil. Tall, with black hair and flashing brown eyes, and a body to swoon over. I thought he was the best thing since sliced bread. He used to stop by my desk to compliment me every morning. By the time he asked me out four months later I was so ripe a plum he had me in bed before you could say ''cheese''.'

'Heavens! And was he a good lover?' Vivien asked, fascinated at the image of her softly spoken, very reserved mother going to bed with a man on a first date.

'Not really. Though I didn't know that at the time. I thought any shortcomings had to be mine. Still, I went eagerly back for more because his looks held a kind of fascination for my body which I didn't have the maturity to ignore. It wasn't till his fiancée swanned into the office one day that my eyes were well and truly opened to the sort of man he was.'

'So what did you do?'

'I found myself a better job and left a much wiser girl. Believe me, the next time a tall, dark and handsome man with flashing eyes set my heart a-flutter he had a darned hard time even getting to first base with me.'

'You gave him the cold shoulder, right?'

'Too right.'

'So what happened to him?'

'I married him.'

Vivien's brown eyes rounded. 'Goodness!'

'What I'm trying to tell you, daughter of mine, is that there's probably any number of men in this world that you might want as a lover, but not too many as your true love. When that chemistry strikes, hold back from it for a while, give yourself time to find out if the object of your desire is worth entrusting your body to, give the relationship a chance to grow on levels other than the sexual one. For it's those other levels that will stand your relationship in good stead in the tough times. You and Earl had nothing going for you but what you had in bed.'

'Which wasn't all that great,' Vivien admitted.

There was a short, sharp silence before Peggy spoke.

'I gather you can't say the same for the time you spent with this Ross person?'

Vivien coloured guiltily. There was no use in pretending any more that what she had felt with Ross that night had been anything like what she'd felt with Earl. Why, it was like comparing a scratchy old record to the very best compact disc.

Her mother said nothing for a moment. 'Have you considered an abortion?' she finally asked.

'Yes.'

'And?'

'I just can't. I know it would be an easy way out, a quick solution. Funnily enough, I've always believed it was a woman's right to make such a decision, and I still do, but somehow, on this occasion, it doesn't feel right. I'm scared, but I...I have to have this baby, Mum. Please...don't ask me to get rid of it.' She threw her

mother a beseeching look, tears welling up in her eyes
again.

Peggy's eyes also flooded. 'As if I would,' she said in
a strangled tone. 'Come here, darling child, and give your
old mother another hug. We'll work things out. Don't you
worry. Everything will be all right.'

Vivien moved home the next day. Her pregnancy was
confirmed two weeks later.

Once over her initial shock, her mother responded by
fussing over Vivien, not allowing her to do anything
around the house. Vivien responded by going into somewhat of a daze.

Most of her days were spent blankly watching television. Her nights, however, were not quite so uneventful,
mostly because of her dreams. They were always of Ross
and herself in a mixed-up version of that fateful night at
Wallaby Creek.

Sometimes they would be on the creek bank, sometimes
in the water, sometimes back in the hotel room. Ross
would be kissing her, touching her, telling her he loved
her. Inevitably, she would wake up before they really
made love, beads of perspiration all over her body. Each
morning, she would get up feeling totally wrung out. That
was till she started having morning sickness as well.

Why, she would ask herself in the bathroom mirror
every day, was she so hell-bent on such a potentially self-
destructive path?

She could not find a sensible, logical answer.

A few days before Christmas, she made another decision about her baby, one which had never been in doubt

at the back of her mind. All that had been in doubt was *when* she was going to do it.

'Dad?' she said that evening after dinner.

Her father looked up from where he was watching a movie on television and reading the evening paper at the same time. 'Yes, love?'

'Would you mind if I made a long-distance call? It doesn't cost so much at night and I promise not to talk for long.'

Now her mother looked up, a frown on her face. 'Who are you ringing, dear?'

'Ross.'

Her father stiffened in his chair. 'What in hell do you want to ring him for? He won't want anything to do with the child, you mark my words.'

'You're probably right,' Vivien returned, the image of Ross's furious departure still stark in her memory. He'd made his feelings quite clear. He never wanted to see her again.

But a few months back, she had done a segment for television on unmarried fathers, and the emotional distress of some of the men had lived with her long afterwards. One of their complaints was that some of the mothers had not even the decency to tell them about their pregnancies. Many had simply not given the fathers any say at all in their decisions to abort, adopt, or to keep their babies. Vivien had been touched by the men's undoubted pain. She knew that she would not be able to live with her conscience if she kept her baby a secret from its father.

A dark thought suddenly insinuated that she might be telling Ross about the baby simply to see him again.

Maybe she wanted the opportunity to bring her erotic dreams to a very real and less frustrating fruition.

Pushing *that* thought agitatedly to the back of her mind, she addressed her frowning parents with a simplicity and apparent certainty she was no longer feeling.

'He has a right to know,' she stated firmly, and threw both her father and mother a stubborn look.

They recognised it as the same look they'd received when they'd advised her, on leaving school, not to try for such a demanding career as television, to do something easier, like teaching.

'You do what you think best, dear,' her mother said with a sigh.

'It'll cause trouble,' her father muttered. 'You mark my words!'

Vivien recklessly ignored her father's last remark, closing the lounge door as she went out into the front hall, where they kept the phone. Her hands were trembling as she picked it up and dialled the operator to help her find Ross's phone number.

Three minutes later she had the number. She dialled again with still quaking fingers, gripping the receiver so tightly against her ear that it was aching already.

No one answered. It rang and rang at the other end, Vivien's disappointment so acute that she could not bring herself to hang up. Then suddenly there was a click and a male voice was on the line.

'Mountainview. Ross Everton speaking.'

Vivien was momentarily distracted by the sounds of merry-making in the background. Loud music and laughter. Clearly a party was in progress.

And why not? she reasoned, swiftly dampening down

a quite unreasonable surge of resentment. Christmas was, after all, less than a few days away. Lots of people were having parties.

She gathered herself and started speaking. 'Ross, this is Vivien here, Vivien Roberts. I...I...' Her voice trailed away, her courage suddenly deserting her. It was so impossible to blurt out her news with all that racket going on in the background.

'I can hardly hear you, Vivien,' Ross returned. 'Look, I'll just go into the library and take this call there. Won't be a moment.'

Vivien was left hanging, quite taken aback that Ross's house would *have* a room called a library. It gave rise to a vision of an old English mansion with panelled walls and deep leather chairs, not the simple country homestead she had envisaged Ross's family living in. She was still somewhat distracted when Ross came back on the line, this time without the party noises to mar his deeply attractive voice. 'Vivien? You're still there?'

'Y...yes.'

There was a short, very electric silence.

'To what honour do I owe this call?' he went on drily. 'You haven't been drinking again, have you?' he added with a sardonic laugh.

'I wish I had,' she muttered under her breath. She hadn't realised how hard this was going to be. Yet what had she expected? That Ross would react to her unexpected call with warmth and pleasure?

'What was that?'

'Nothing.' Her tone became brisk and businesslike. 'I'm sorry to bother you during your Christmas party, but I have something to tell you which simply can't wait.'

'Oh?' Wariness in his voice. 'Something unpleasant by the sound of it.'

'*You* may think so.' Her tone was becoming sharper by the second, fuelled by a terrible feeling of coming doom. He was going to hate her news. Simply hate it!

'Vivien, you're not going to tell me you have contracted some unmentionable disease, are you?'

'Not unless you refer to pregnancy in such a way,' she snapped back.

His inward suck of breath seemed magnified as it rushed down the line to her already pained ears.

Vivien squeezed her eyes tightly shut. You blithering idiot, she berated herself. You tactless, clumsy blithering idiot! 'Ross,' she resumed tightly, 'I'm sorry I blurted it out like that. I...I—'

'What happened?' he said in a voice that showed amazing control. 'You did say, after all, that you were on the Pill. Did you forget to take it, is that it?'

She expelled a ragged sigh. 'Yes...'

Once again, there was an unnerving silence on the line before he resumed speaking. 'And you're sure I'm the father?' he asked, but without any accusation.

'Quite sure.'

'I see.'

'Ross, I...I'm not ringing because I want anything from you. Not money, or anything. I realise that I'm entirely to blame. It's just that I thought you had the right to know, then to make your own decision as to whether you want to...to share in your child's life. It's entirely up to you. I'll understand whatever decision you make.'

'You mean you're going to *have* my baby?' he rasped,

shock and something else in his voice. Or maybe not. Maybe just shock.

'You don't want me to,' she said, wretchedness in her heart.

'What I want is obviously irrelevant. Does your family know you're going to have a baby?'

'Yes. I'm ringing from their place now. I moved back home a couple of weeks ago.'

'And how did they react?'

'They weren't thrilled at first, but they're resigned now, and supportive.'

'Hmm. Does Earl know?'

'Of course not!'

'Don't bite my head off, Vivien. You wouldn't be the first woman who tried to use another man's baby to get back the man she really wants. In the circumstances, I doubt you'd have had much trouble in passing the child off as his, since the father is his dead ringer.'

Vivien was shocked that Ross would even *think* of such a thing.

'Is that why you're having the baby, Vivien?' he continued mercilessly. 'Because you're hoping it will look like the man you love?'

She gasped. 'You're sick, do you know that?'

'Possibly. But I had to ask.'

'*Why?*'

'So that I can make rational decisions. I don't think you have any idea what your news has done to my life, Vivien.'

'What…what do you mean?'

'I mean that it isn't a Christmas party we're having here tonight. It's an engagement party. *Mine.*'

Vivien's mind went blank for a second. When it resumed operation and the reality of the situation sank in, any initial sympathy she might have felt for Ross was swiftly replaced by a sharp sense of betrayal.

'I see,' she bit out acidly.

'Do you?'

'Of course. You slept with me at the same time as you were courting another woman. You lied to me when you came after me, Ross. You didn't want a real relationship. All you wanted was a final fling before you settled down to your real life.'

'I wouldn't put it that way exactly,' he drawled.

'Then what way would you put it?'

'Let's just say I found you sexually irresistible. Once I had you in my arms, I simply couldn't stop.'

Vivien was appalled by the flush of heat that washed over her skin as she thought of how she had felt in *his* arms. She couldn't seem to stop either. Once she might have fancied she had fallen in love with Ross. Now she had another word for it, supplied by her mother.

Chemistry, it was called, the same chemistry that had originally propelled her so willingly into Earl's arms. Though Earl had had another word for it. *Lust!*

Vivien shuddered. God, but she hated to think her mind and heart could be totally fooled by her body. It was demeaning to her intelligence.

Men weren't fooled, though. They knew the difference between love and lust. They even seemed capable of feeling both at the same time. Ross had probably kept on loving this woman he was about to marry, all the while he was lusting after *her*.

'Let's hope you don't run into someone like me after

you get married in that case,' she flung at Ross with a degree of venom.

'I won't be getting married, Vivien,' he said quite calmly. 'At least…not now, and not to Becky.'

Vivien's anger turned to a flustered outrage. Not for herself this time, but for the poor wronged woman who wore Ross's ring. 'But…but you can't break your engagement just like that. That…that's cruel!'

'It would be crueller to go through with it. Becky deserves more than a husband who's going to be the father of another woman's baby. I wouldn't do that to her. I've loved Becky all my life,' he stated stiffly. 'We're neighbours as well. I'm deeply sorry that I have to hurt her at all. But this is a case of being cruel to be kind.'

'Oh, I feel so guilty,' Vivien cried. 'I should never have rung, never have told you.'

'Perhaps. But what's done is done. And now we must think of the child. When can I come down and see you?'

'See me?' she repeated, her head whirling.

'How about Boxing Day? I really can't get away from here before Christmas. Give me your parents' address and telephone number.'

Stunned, she did as he asked. He jotted down the particulars, then repeated them back to her.

'Do me a favour, will you, Vivien?' he added brusquely. 'Don't tell your parents about the engagement. It's going to be tough enough making them accept me as the father of their grandchild without my having an advance black mark against my name. However, you'd better let them know about my remarkable resemblance to lover-boy. I don't think I could stand any more people calling me Earl by mistake.'

He dragged in then exhaled a shuddering breath. 'Ah, well…I'd better go and drop my bombshell. Something tells me this party is going to break up rather early. See you Boxing Day, Vivien. Look after yourself.'

Vivien stared down into the dead receiver for several seconds before putting it shakily back into its cradle. Normally a clear thinker, she found it hard to grasp how she really felt about what had just happened. Her emotions seemed to have scrambled her brains.

Ross, she finally accepted, was the key to her confusion. Ross…who had just destroyed the picture she had formed of him in her mind.

He was not some smitten suitor who had chased after her with an almost adolescent passion, ready to throw himself at her feet. He was the man she had first met, an intriguing mixture of sophisticate and macho male, a man who was capable of going after what he wanted with the sort of ruthlessness that could inspire a brother's hatred. He was, quite clearly, another rat!

No…she conceded slowly. Not quite.

A rat would have told her get lost. Her *and* her baby.

A rat would not have broken his engagement.

A rat would not be coming down to see her, concerned with her parents' opinion of him.

So what was he?

Vivien wasn't at all sure, except about one thing.

He was *not* in love with her.

He was in love with a woman named Becky.

Now why did that hurt so darned much?

CHAPTER SEVEN

'HE'S here,' Peggy hissed, drawing back the living-room drapes to have a better look. 'Goodness, but you should see the Range Rover he's pulled up in. Looks brand new. Can't be one of those farmers who're doing really badly, then.'

Lionel grunted from his favourite armchair. 'Don't you believe it, Mother. Graziers live on large overdrafts. Most of them are going down the tubes.'

'Well, I'd rather see my Vivien married to an overdraft*ee* than that overdraft*er* she was living with. Heavens, but I could not stand that man. Oh, my goodness, but this fellow does look like Earl. Taller, though, and fitter looking. Hmm… Yes, I can see why Vivien was bowled over. He's a bit of all right.'

'Peggy!' Lionel exclaimed, startled enough to put down his newspaper. 'What's got into you, talking like that? And don't start romanticising about our Vivien getting married just because she's having a baby. She's never been one to follow convention. Not that this Ross chap will want to marry her anyway. Young men don't marry girls these days for that reason.'

'He's not so young…'

'What's that?' Lionel levered himself out of his chair and came to his wife's side, peering with her through the lacy curtains. By this time, Ross was making his way through the front gate, his well-honed frame coolly

88

dressed for the heat in white shorts and a pale blue polo shirt, white socks and blue and white striped Reeboks on his feet.

Lionel frowned. 'Must be thirty if he's a day.'

'Well, our Vivien *is* twenty-five,' Peggy argued.

'What on earth are you two doing?' the girl herself said with more than a touch of exasperation.

They both swung round, like guilty children found with their hands in the cookie jar.

The front doorbell rang.

Vivien folded her arms. 'If that's Ross why don't you just let him in instead of spying on him?'

'We—er—um…' came Peggy's lame mumblings till she gathered herself and changed from defence to attack.

'Vivien! Surely you're not going to let Ross see you wearing that horrible old housecoat? Go and put something decent on. And while you're at it, put some lipstick on as well. And run a brush through your hair. You look as if you've just got out of bed.'

'I *have* just got out of bed,' she returned irritably. 'And I have no intention of dolling myself up for Ross. He's not my boyfriend.'

'He *is* the father of your baby,' Lionel reminded her.

'More's the pity,' she muttered. Having been given a few days to think over the events surrounding that fateful weekend, Vivien had decided Ross was a rat after all. At least where women were concerned. He'd known she'd been upset about Earl that night, had known he himself had been on the verge of asking another woman to be his bride, one he *claimed* to have loved for years. Yet what had he done? Cold-bloodedly taken advantage of her vulnerability by seducing her, making her forget her conscience and then her pill!

'Vivien,' her mother said sternly, 'it was *your* idea to call Ross and tell him about the baby, which was a very brave and adult decision, but now you're acting like a child. Go and make yourself presentable *immediately*!'

Vivien took one look at her mother's determined face and knew this was not the moment to get on her high horse. Besides, her mother was right. She was acting appallingly. Still, she had felt rotten all day, with a queasy stomach and a dull headache, as she had the day before. She hadn't even been able to enjoy her Christmas dinner, due to a case of morning sickness which lasted all day. If this was what being pregnant was like then it was strictly for the birds!

'Oh, all right,' she muttered, just as the front doorbell rang for the second time. 'You'd better go and let him in. Something tells me Ross Everton is not in the habit of waiting for anything.'

She flounced off, feeling ashamed of herself, but seemingly unable to do anything about the way she was acting. On top of her physical ills, the news of Ross's engagement had left her feeling betrayed and bitter and even more disillusioned about men than she already had. It was as though suddenly there were no dreams any more.

No dreams. No Prince Charming. No hope.

Life had become drearily disappointing and utterly, utterly depressing.

Vivien threw open her wardrobe and drew out the first thing her hands landed on, a strappy lime sundress which showed a good deal of bare flesh. For a second, she hesitated. But only for a second. She had always favoured bright, extrovert clothes. Her wardrobe was full of them. Maybe wearing fluorescent green would cheer her up.

Tossing aside all her clothes, she drew on fresh bikini briefs before stepping into the dress and drawing it up over her hourglass figure. With wry accession to her mother's wishes, she brushed her dishevelled hair into disciplined waves before applying a dash of coral gloss to her lips.

The mirror told her she looked far better than she felt, the vibrant green a perfect foil for her pale skin and jet-black hair. Yet when her eyes dropped to her full breasts straining against the thin cotton, Ross's words leapt back into her mind.

'I found you sexually irresistible...'

The words pained her, as Earl's words had pained her.

'It was only lust,' *he* had said.

Vivien couldn't get the dress off quickly enough, choosing instead some loose red and white spotted Bermuda shorts with a flowing white over-shirt to cover her womanly curves. The last thing she wanted today was Ross looking at her with desire in his eyes. Suddenly, she found her own sex appeal a hateful thing that stood between herself and real happiness.

Reefing a tissue out of the box, she wiped savagely at her glossed lips, though the resultant effect was not what she wanted. Sure, the lipstick was gone, but the rubbing had left her lips quite red and swollen, giving her wide mouth a full, sultry look.

'Damn,' she muttered.

'Vivien,' came her mother's voice through the bedroom door, 'when you're ready you'll find us on the back patio. Your father and Ross are having a beer together out there.'

Vivien blinked. Dad was having a beer with Ross? Already? How astonishing. He only ever offered a beer to his best mates. Perhaps he needed a beer himself, she decided. It had to be an awkward situation for him, entertaining Ross, trying to find something to talk to him about.

I should be out there, she thought guiltily.

But still she lingered, afraid to leave the sanctuary of her bedroom, afraid of what she would still see in Ross's eyes when they met hers, afraid of what she might *not* see.

Vivien violently shook her head. This was crazy! One moment she didn't want him to want her. Then the next she did. It was all too perverse for words!

Self-disgust finally achieved what filial duty and politeness could not. Vivien marched from the room, bitterly resolved to conquer these vacillating desires that kept invading her mind and body. Ross wanted to talk to her about their coming child? Well, that was all he'd ever get from her in future. Talk! She had no intention of letting him worm his way past her physical defences ever again.

She stomped down the hall, through the kitchen and out on to the back patio, letting the wire door bang as she went. The scenario of a totally relaxed Ross seated cosily between her parents around the patio table, sipping a cool beer and looking too darned handsome for words, did nothing for her growing irritation.

'Ah, here she is now,' her father said expansively. 'Ross was just telling us that he's not normally a sheep farmer. He's simply helping out at home till his father gets on his feet again. He flies helicopters for a living.

Mustering cattle. Own your own business, didn't you say, Ross?'

'That's right, Mr Roberts. I've built up quite a clientele over the last few years. Mustering on horseback is definitely on the way out, though some people like to call us chopper cowboys.'

'Chopper cowboys... Now that's a clever way of putting it. And do call me Lionel, my boy. No point in being formal, in the circumstances, is there?' he added with a small laugh.

Ross smiled that crooked smile that made him look far too much like Earl. 'I guess not,' he drawled, and lifted the beer to his lips.

'But isn't that rather a dangerous occupation?' Peggy piped up with a worried frown.

'Only if you're unskilled,' Ross returned. 'Or careless. I'm usually neither.' He slanted Vivien a ruefully sardonic look that changed her inner agitation into an icy fury.

'Accidents do happen though, don't they?' she said coldly.

'Now don't go getting all prickly on us, love,' Lionel intervened. 'We all know that neither of you had any intention of having a baby together, but you *are*, and Ross here has at least been decent enough to come all this way to meet us and reassure us he'll do everything he can to support you and the child. You should be grateful that he's prepared to do the right thing.'

Vivien counted to ten, then came forward to pick up an empty glass and pour herself some orange juice out of the chilled cask on the table. 'I *am* grateful,' she said stiffly. 'I only hope no one here suggests that we get mar-

ried. I won't be marrying anyone for any reason other than
true love.'

She lifted her glass and eyes at the same time, locking
visual swords with Ross over the rim. But she wasn't the
only one who could hide her innermost feelings behind a
facial façade. He eyed her back without so much as a
flicker of an eyelash, his cool blue eyes quite unflappable
in their steady regard.

'Believe me, Vivien,' came his smooth reply, 'neither
will I.'

An electric silence descended on the group as Vivien
and Ross glared at each other in mutual defiance.

'Perhaps, Mother...' Lionel said, scraping back his
chair to stand up. 'Perhaps we should leave these two
young people to have a private chat.'

'Good idea, dear,' Peggy agreed, and stood up also.
'Here, Vivien, use my chair. Now be careful. Don't spill
your drink as you sit down.'

Vivien rolled her eyes while her mother treated her like
a cross between a child and an invalid.

'Will you be staying for dinner, Ross?' Peggy asked
before she left.

Ross glanced at his wristwatch which showed five to
six. He looked up and smiled. 'If it's not too much trouble.'

'No trouble at all. We're only having cold meats and
salad. Left-overs, I'm afraid, from yesterday's Christmas
feast.'

'I love left-overs,' he assured her.

Once her parents had gone inside, Vivien heaved a
heavy sigh.

'Not feeling well, Viv?' Ross ventured.

She shot him a savage look. 'Don't call me that.'

'What? "Viv"?'

'Yes.'

'Why?'

She shrugged irritably.

'Did Earl call you that?'

'No,' she lied.

He raised his eyebrows, but said nothing.

'Look, Ross, I'm just out of sorts today, OK?' Vivien burst out. 'It isn't all beer and skittles being pregnant, you know.'

'No, I don't know,' he said with a rueful note in his voice. 'But I guess I'm going to find out over the next few months. Something tells me you're a vocal type of girl.'

She darted him a dry look. 'If by that you mean I'm a shrew or a whinger then you couldn't be further from the truth. It's just that I didn't expect to be this sick all the time. I guess I'll get used to it in time. Though I'm damned if I'll get used to my mother's fussing,' she finished with a grimace of true frustration.

'You're going to live here?'

'Where else? I had no intention of staying on in Earl's flat. Besides, I'm unemployed now and I wouldn't have enough money for the rent anyway, so I have to stay here. There's no other alternative.'

'You could come home with me,' he suggested blandly.

Her mouth dropped open, then snapped shut. 'Oh, don't be ridiculous!'

'I'm not being ridiculous. Dad wants to meet you, and I'd like to have you.'

'I'll just bet you would,' she shot at him quite nastily.

Both his eyebrows shot up again. 'You have a dirty mind, Vivien, my dear.'

'Maybe it's the company I'm keeping.'

Anger glittered in his eyes. 'Perhaps you would prefer to be with a man who used you quite ruthlessly then discarded you like an old worn-out shoe!'

Vivien paled. Her bottom lip trembled.

'God,' Ross groaned immediately, placing his beer glass down on the table with a ragged thud. 'I'm sorry, Vivien. Deeply, sincerely sorry. That was a rotten thing to say.'

'Yes,' she rasped, tears pricking at her eyes.

She stared blindly down into her orange juice, amazed at the pain Ross's words had produced. There she'd been lately, almost agreeing with her mother that she had never loved Earl. But she must have, for this reminder of his treachery to hurt so much.

Or maybe she was just in an over-emotional state, being pregnant and all. She had heard pregnancy made some women quite irrational.

With several blinks and a sigh, she glanced up, only to be shocked by the degree of bleak apology on Ross's face. He really was very sorry, it seemed.

Now she felt guilty. For she hadn't exactly been Little Miss Politeness since joining him.

'I'm sorry too, Ross,' she said sincerely, 'This can't be easy for you either. I won't pretend that I'm thrilled at finding out you only looked upon me as a "bit on the side", so to speak, but who am I to judge? My behaviour was hardly without fault. I was probably using you that night as much as you were using me, so perhaps we should try to forgive each other's shortcomings and start all over again, shall we?'

He stared at her. 'You really mean that?'

'Of course. You're the father of my baby. We should at least try to be friends. I can also see it's only sensible that I should come out to meet your family, though I really can't stay with you for my entire pregnancy. Surely *you* can see that?'

'Actually, no, I can't.'

She made an exasperated sound. 'It wouldn't be right. I've never been a leaner. I have to make my own way.'

'That might have been all right when it was just you, Vivien,' he pointed out. 'But soon you'll have a child to support. You have no job and, I would guess, few savings. And, before you jump down my throat for being presumptuous, I'm only saying that because you're not old enough to have accrued a fortune.'

'I'm twenty-five!'

'Positively ancient. And you've been working how long? Four years at most?'

'Something like that...'

'Women never get paid as much as men in the media. Besides, in your line of work you would have had to spend a lot on clothes.'

'Yes...'

'See? It doesn't take a genius to guess at your financial position. Besides, I have a proposition to make to you.'

This brought a wary, narrow-eyed glare. 'Oh, yes?'

'Nothing like that,' he dismissed. 'My father has just come home from a stay in hospital where he's been having therapy. I have engaged a private therapist who specialises in after-stroke care to visit regularly, but there are still times when he needs someone to read to him and talk to him, or just sit with him.'

'A paid companion, you mean?'

'Yes. Something like that. Do you think you might be interested? It would kill two birds with one stone. Dad would get to know the mother of his grandchild and vice versa. And you'd feel a bit more useful than you're obviously feeling now.'

'Mmm.' Vivien gnawed away at her bottom lip. 'I've applied for social security…'

'No matter. You can either cancel it or I'll put your wages into a trust fund for the child.'

She wrinkled her nose. 'I'd rather cancel it.'

'*You would.*'

She bristled at his exasperated tone. 'Meaning?'

'You're too proud, Vivien. And too honest. You must learn that life is a jungle and sometimes the good get it in the neck.'

'Are you saying you have no pride? That you're not honest?'

A shadow passed across his eyes, turning them to a wintry grey for a second. But they were soon back to their bright icy blue. 'Let's just say that I *have* been known to go after what I want with a certain one-eyed determination.'

She gave him a long, considering look, trying not to let his physical appeal rattle her thought processes. It was hard, though. He was a devastatingly sexy man, much sexier than Earl. Oh, their looks were still remarkably similar—on the surface. But Ross had an inner energy, a raw vitality that shone through in every look he gave her, every move he made. Even sitting there casually in a deckchair with his legs stretched out, ankles crossed, he exuded an animal-like sensuality that sent tickles up and down her spine.

'Have you thought up this companion job simply to get me into a position where you can seduce me again?' she asked point-blank.

He seemed startled for a moment before recovering his cool poise. 'No,' he said firmly, and looked her straight in the eye. 'Believe me when I say there will *not* be a repeat performance of what happened that night out at Wallaby Creek.'

He sounded as if he was telling the truth, she realised with a degree of surprise. And disappointment. The latter reaction sparked self-irritation. If *he* had managed to bring this unfortunate chemistry between them under control, then why couldn't *she*?

'Are you two ready to eat?' her mother called through the wire door. 'It's all set out.'

'Coming,' they chorused.

Thank God for the interruption, Vivien thought as she and Ross stood up.

'Vivien?' he said, taking her elbow to stop her before she could walk away.

'Yes?'

'Are you going to take me up on the offer or not?'

She tried to concentrate on all the common-sense reasons why it was a good idea, and not on the way his touch was making her pulse-rate do a tango within her veins.

'Vivien?' he probed again.

Swallowing, she lifted her dark eyes to his light blue ones, hoping like hell that he couldn't read her mind. Or her body language.

'If you trust me in this,' he said softly, 'I will not abuse that trust.'

Maybe, she thought. But could she say the same for her own strength of will? She'd shown little enough self-control once she'd found herself in his arms in the past. What if he'd been lying earlier about why he wanted her in his home? What if he was lying *now*? Men often lied to satisfy their lust. Now that she was already pregnant and his engagement was off, what was to stop Ross from using her to satisfy his sexual needs? How easy it would be with her already under his roof...

'Vivien!' her mother called again. 'What's keeping you?' Her face appeared at the wire door. 'Come on, now, love. I've got a nice salad all ready. You must eat, you know, since you're eating for two. And I've put out the vitamins the doctor suggested you have. Ross, don't take any nonsense from her and bring her in here right away.'

'Sure thing, Mrs Roberts.'

He smiled at the pained look on Vivien's face. 'Well? What do you say? Will you give it a try for a few months?'

A few months...

Something warned her that was too long, too dangerous.

'One month,' she compromised. 'Then we'll see...'

Still looking into his eyes, Vivien would have had to be blind not to see the depth of Ross's satisfaction. Her stomach turned over and she tore her eyes away. What have I done? she worried.

As he opened the wire door and guided her into the large, airy kitchen, the almost triumphant expression on Ross's face sent an old saying into her mind.

'"Will you walk into my parlour?" said a spider to a fly..."'

CHAPTER EIGHT

'WHAT did Mum say to you?' Vivien demanded to know as soon as the Range Rover moved out of sight of her waving parents.

Ross darted a sideways glance at her, his expression vague. 'When?'

'When she called you back to the front gate just now.' She eyed Ross suspiciously. 'She isn't trying to put any pressure on you to marry me, is she?'

'Don't be paranoid, Vivien. Your mother simply asked me not to speed, to remember that I had a very precious cargo aboard.'

'Oh, good grief! That woman's becoming impossible. God knows what she'll be like by the time I actually *have* this baby.'

'Speaking of the baby, are you feeling better today?'

'No,' she grumped. 'I feel positively rotten.'

'Really? You look fantastic. That green suits you.'

Vivien stiffened, recalling how she had argued with her mother over what she should wear this morning. In the end she had given in to her mother's view that she should dress the way she always dressed, not run around hiding her figure in tent dresses and voluminous tops.

But now Vivien wasn't so sure wearing such a bare dress was wise. She hadn't forgotten the way Ross had looked yesterday when she'd agreed to go home with him

for a while. The last thing she wanted to do was be pro-
vocative.

'I thought you said that you wanted us to start all over
again,' Ross reminded her, 'that we should try to be
friends. If this is your idea of being friendly then city folk
sure as hell are different from country.'

His words made Vivien feel guilty. She was being as
bitchy today as she had been yesterday, and it wasn't all
because she felt nauseous. When Ross had shown up this
morning, looking cool and handsome all in white, she
hadn't been able to take her eyes off him. Her only defence against her fluttering heart had been sharp words
and a cranky countenance.

Vivien shook her head. Her vulnerability to this chemistry business was the very devil. It played havoc with
one's conscience, making her want to invite things that
she knew were not in her best interests. Maybe some people could quite happily satisfy their lust without any disastrous consequences. But Vivien feared that if she did
so with Ross she might become emotionally involved with
him.

And where would that leave her, loving a man who
didn't love her back, a man whose heart had been given
to another woman? It wasn't as though there was any hope
of his marrying her, either. He'd made his ideas on that
quite clear.

Still, none of these inner torturous thoughts were any
excuse for her poor manners, and she knew it.

'I'm sorry, Ross,' she apologised. 'I'll be in a better
humour shortly. This yucky feeling usually wears off by
mid-morning.'

He smiled over at her. 'I'll look forward to it.'

They fell into a companionable silence after that, Vivien soon caught up by the changing scenery as they made their way up the Blue Mountains and through Katoomba. She had been the driver during this section when she and Irving had made the trip out to Wallaby Creek, and the driver certainly didn't see as much as the passenger. Oddly enough, the curving road did not exacerbate her slightly queasy stomach. In fact she was soon distracted from her sickness with watching the many and varied vistas.

Despite being built on at regular intervals, the mountain terrain still gave one the feeling of its being totally untouched in places. The rock-faces dropped down into great gorges, the distant hillsides covered with a virgin bush so wild and dense that Vivien understood only too well why bushwalkers every year became lost in them. She shuddered to think what would happen to the many isolated houses if a bush-fire took hold.

'It's very dry, isn't it?' she remarked at last with worry in her voice.

'Sure is. My father says it's the worst drought since the early forties.'

'How old *is* your father, Ross?' Vivien asked.

'Sixty-three.'

'Still too young to die,' she murmured softly. 'And you?'

'I'll be thirty-one next birthday. What is this, twenty questions?'

Vivien shrugged. 'I think I should know a little about your family before I arrive, don't you?'

'Yes. I suppose that's only reasonable. Fire away, then.'

'Who else is there at Mountainview besides you and

your father and Gavin? I presume you three men don't fend for yourselves.'

He laughed. 'You presume right. If we did, we'd starve. We have Helga to look after us.'

'Helga... She sounds formidable.'

'She is. Came to us as a nurse when Mum became terminally ill. After she died, Helga stayed on, saying we couldn't possibly cope without her. I was twelve at the time. Gavin was only seven. He looks upon Helga as a second mother.'

'And you? Do you look upon her as a second mother?'

'Heaven forbid. The woman's a martinet. No, only Gavin softens that woman's heart. She'd make an excellent sergeant in the army. Still, she does the work of three women so I can't complain. Keeps the whole house spick and span, does all the washing and cooking and ironing, and still has time left over to knit us all the most atrocious jumpers. I have a drawer full of them.'

'Oh, she sounds sweet.' Vivien laughed.

'She means well, I suppose. She's devoted to Mountainview. The house, that is. Not the sheep.'

'Is it a big house? I got the impression it was on the phone.'

'Too damned big. Built when graziers were nothing more than Pitt Street farmers who used their station properties as country retreats to impress their city friends. We don't even use some sections of the house. Dad gets a team of cleaners in once a year to spring-clean. When they're finished, they cover the furniture in half the rooms with dust-cloths then lock the doors.'

'Goodness, it sounds like a mansion. How many rooms has it got?'

'Forty-two.'

Vivien blinked over at his amused face. 'You're pulling my leg.'

He glanced down at her shapely ankles. 'Unfortunately, no.'

'Forty-two,' she repeated in amazement. 'And you only have the one woman to keep house?'

'In the main. We hire extra staff if we're having a party or a lot of visitors. And there's Stan and Dave.'

'Who are they?'

'General farmhands. Or rouseabouts, if you prefer. But they don't live in the main house. They have their own quarters. Still, they do look after the gardens, so you're likely to run into them occasionally. Of course, the place is a lot busier during shearing, but that won't be till March.'

'March...' Vivien wondered if she would still be there in March. She turned her head slowly to look at Ross. In profile, he looked nothing like Earl at all, yet her stomach still executed a telling flutter.

'Do...do you think Helga will like me?' Vivien asked hesitantly.

'I don't see why not.'

Vivien frowned. Men could be so naïve at times. If Helga had been fond of Ross's Becky then she wouldn't be very welcoming to the woman who'd been responsible for breaking the girl's heart.

But *was* it broken? she wondered. Ross had confessed his long love for the woman he'd planned to marry, but Vivien knew nothing of the woman herself, or her feelings.

'Ross...'

'Mmm?'

'Tell me about Becky.'

He stiffened in his seat, his hands tightening around the wheel. 'For God's sake, Vivien...'

She bristled. 'For God's sake what? Surely I have a right to know something about the woman you were planning to marry, the woman you were sleeping with the same time you were sleeping with me?'

'I was not sleeping with Becky,' he ground out. 'I have *never* slept with Becky.'

Vivien stared over at him. 'But...but...'

'Oh, I undoubtedly would have,' he confessed testily. 'After we were properly engaged.'

Vivien could not deny that there was a certain amount of elation mixed in with her astonishment at this news. She had hated to think Ross had behaved as badly as Earl. Not that his behaviour had been impeccable. But at least he hadn't been sleeping with two women at the same time. Though, to be honest, Vivien did find his admission a touch strange.

'I'm not sure I understand,' she said with a puzzled frown. 'If you've always loved this Becky, then why haven't you made love to her? Why were you waiting till you were engaged?'

His sigh was irritable. 'It's difficult to explain.'

'*Try*,' she insisted.

He shot her an exasperated glance. 'Why do you want to know? Why do you care? You're not in love with me. What difference can it possibly make?'

'I want to know.'

'You are an incredibly stubborn woman!'

'So my mother has always told me.'

'She didn't tell *me* that,' he muttered.

'Didn't she? Well, what did she tell you, then? Were you lying to me back in Sydney whe—?'

'Oh, for pity's sake give it a rest, will you, Vivien? We've a tiresome trip ahead and you're going on like a Chinese water torture. God! Why I damned well...' He broke off, lancing her with another reproachful glare. 'You would have to be the most infuriating female I have ever met!'

Vivien's temper flared. 'Is that so? You certainly didn't find me infuriating once you got my clothes off, did you? You found me pretty fascinating then all right!'

He fixed her with an oddly chilling glance as he pulled over to the side of the road and cut the engine.

'Yes,' he grated out, then thumped the steering-wheel. 'I did. Is that what you want to hear? How I couldn't get enough of you that night? How I wouldn't have stopped at all if I hadn't flaked out with sheer exhaustion?'

He scooped in then exhaled a shuddering breath, taking a few seconds to compose himself. 'Now what else do you want to know...? Ah, yes, why I haven't slept with Becky? Well, perhaps my reasons might be clearer if I tell you she's only twenty-one years old, and a virgin to boot. Convent-educated. A total innocent where men are concerned. Somehow it didn't seem right to take that innocence away till my ring was on her finger. So I waited...

'It's just as well I did, in the circumstances,' he finished pointedly.

Vivien sat there in a bleak silence, her heart a great lump of granite in her chest. Heavy and hard and cold. My God, he had really just spelt it out for her, hadn't he?

She could be taken within hours of their first meeting. For *she* had no innocence to speak of, no virtue to be treasured or respected. She was little better than a slut in his eyes, fit only to be lusted after, to be *screwed*!

Not so this girl he loved. She was to be treated like spun glass, put up on a pedestal, looked at but not touched, not ruthlessly seduced as he'd seduced her over and over that night.

She pressed a curled fist against her lips lest a groan of dismay escape, turning her face away to stare blindly through the passenger window. Well, at least this would give her a weapon to use against herself every time that hated chemistry raised its ugly head. She would only have to remember exactly how she stood in Ross's eyes for those unwanted desires to be frozen to nothingness. She would feel as chilled towards him as she did at this very moment.

'Haven't you any other questions you want answered?' Ross asked in a flat voice.

'No,' was all she could manage.

'In that case I'll put some music on. We've a long drive ahead of us…'

They stopped a couple of times along the way, at roadside cafés which served meals as well as petrol. Each time she climbed out of the cabin Vivien was struck by the heat and was only too glad to be underway again under the cooling fan of the vehicle's air-conditioning.

Vivien stayed quiet after their earlier upsetting encounter, even though the scenery didn't provide her bleak wretchedness with any distractions. The countryside was really quite monotonous once they were out on the

Western plains. Nothing but paddock after flat paddock of brown grass, dotted with the occasional clump of trees under which slept some straggly-looking sheep. Even the towns seemed the same, just bigger versions of Wallaby Creek.

They were driving along shortly after two, the heat above the straight bitumen road forming a shimmering lake, when Vivien got the shock of her life. A huge grey kangaroo suddenly appeared right out of the mirage in front of them, leaping across the road. Ross braked, but he still hit it a glancing blow, though not enough to stop its flight to safety.

Vivien stared as the 'roo went clean over the barbed-wire fence at the side of the road and off across the paddock. Within seconds it had disappeared.

'That's the first kangaroo I've ever seen, outside a zoo!' she exclaimed, propelled out of her earlier depression by excitement at such an unexpected sight. 'I'm glad we didn't hurt it.'

'It'd take more than a bump to hurt one of those big mongrels.' Ross scowled before accelerating away again.

'Why do you call it that?' she objected. 'It's a beautiful animal.'

'Typical city opinion. I suppose you think rabbits are nice, cuddly, harmless little creatures as well?'

'Of course.'

'Then you've never met twenty thousand of the little beggars, munching their way through acres of your top grazing land. The only reason the sheep stations out here haven't got a problem with them at the moment is because there's a drought. Come the rain and they'll plague up, as they always do. The worst thing the English ever did to Australia was import the damned rabbit!'

'Well, you don't have to get all steamed up about it with me,' she pointed out huffily. 'It's not my fault!'

Suddenly he looked across and grinned at her, a wide, cheeky grin that was nothing like Earl would ever indulge in. She couldn't help it. She grinned back, and in that split second she knew she not only desired this man, but she liked him as well. Far too much.

Her grin faded, depression returning to take the place of pleasure. If only Ross genuinely returned the liking. If only she could inspire a fraction of the respect this Becky did...

'What have I done *now*?' he groaned frustratedly.

'Nothing,' she muttered. 'Nothing.'

'I don't seem to have to do anything to upset you, do I? What was it? Did I smile at you like Earl, is that it? Go on, you can tell me. I'm a big boy. I can take it!'

She shrank from his sarcastic outburst, turning her face away. What could she say to him? No, you remind me less and less of Earl with each passing moment...

'Don't you dare give me that silent treatment again, Vivien,' he snapped. 'I can't stand it.'

She sighed and turned back towards him. 'This isn't going to work out, is it, Ross?'

His mouth thinned stubbornly. 'It will, if you'll just give it a chance. Besides, what's your alternative—eight months of your mother's fussing?'

Vivien actually shuddered.

'See? At least I won't fuss over you. And neither will the rest of the people at Mountainview. They have too much to do. You'll be expected to pull your own weight out here, pregnant or not. That's what it's like in the country. You're not an invalid and you won't be treated like one.'

'Do you think that will bother me? I'm not lazy, Ross. I'm a worker too.'

'Then what *is* beginning to bother you? What have I said to make you look at me with such unhappy eyes?'

'I...I really wanted us to become friends.'

'And you think I don't?'

'Friends respect each other.'

He frowned over at her. 'I respect you.'

'No, you don't.'

'God, Vivien, what is this? Do you think I subscribe to that old double standard about sex? Do you think I think you're tainted somehow because you went to bed with me?'

'Yes,' she told him point-blank. 'If you didn't think like that, you'd have slept with Becky and to hell with her so-called innocence. Virginity is not a prize, Ross. It was only valued in the olden days because it assured the bridegroom that his bride would not have venereal disease. Making love is the most wonderful expression of love and affection that can exist between a man and a woman. Yet you backed away from it with the woman you claim you love in favour of it with a perfect stranger, in favour of a "city broad who probably knows more counter-moves than a chess champion". If that sounds as if you respect me then I'm a Dutchman's uncle!'

His face paled visibly, but he kept his eyes on the road ahead. 'That's not how it was, Vivien,' he said tautly.

'Oh?' she scoffed. 'Then how *was* it, Ross?'

'One day I might tell you,' he muttered. 'But for now I think you're forgetting a little something.'

'What?'

'The baby. *Our* baby. It's not the child's fault that he or she is going to be born. The least we can do is provide it with a couple of parents who aren't constantly at each other's throats. I realise I'm not the father you would have chosen for your child, Vivien. Neither am I yet able to fully understand your decision to actually go ahead with this pregnancy. I'm still to be convinced that it has nothing to do with my likeness to the man you're in love with.

'No, don't say a word!' he growled when she went to protest this assumption. 'You might not even recognise your own motives as yet. We all have dark and devious sides, some that remain hidden even to ourselves. But I will not have an innocent child suffer for the perversity of its parents. We're going to be mature about all this, Vivien. *You're* going to be mature. I want no more of your swinging moods or your wild, way-off accusations. You are to treat me with the same decency and respect that I will accord you. Or, by God, I'm going to lay you over my knee and whop that luscious backside of yours. Do I make myself clear?'

She eyed him fiercely, seething inside with a bitter resentment. Who did he think he was, telling her how to behave, implying that she had been acting like an immature idiot, threatening her with physical violence? As for dark and devious sides...he sure as hell had his fair share!

But aside from all that, Vivien could see that he *was* making *some* sense, despite his over-the-top threats. He even made her feel a little guilty. She hadn't really been thinking much about the baby's future welfare. She'd been consumed by her own ambivalent feelings for the man seated beside her. One moment she was desperate for him to like her, the next he was provoking her into a quite irrational anger, making her want to lash out at him. Right at this moment she would have liked to indulge in a bit of physical violence of her own!

Yes, but that's because you simply want to get your hands on him again, came a sinister voice from deep inside.

She stiffened.

'And you can cut out that outraged innocence act too!' he snapped, darting her a vicious glance. 'You're about as innocent as a vampire. *And* about as lethal! So I suggest you keep those pearly white teeth of yours safely within those blood-red lips for the remainder of this journey. For, if you open them again, I swear to you, Vivien, I'll forget that promise I made to you yesterday and give you another dose of what you've obviously been missing to have turned you into such a shrew. I'm sure you're quite capable of closing those big brown eyes of yours and pretending I'm Earl once more. And I'm just as capable of thoroughly enjoying myself in his stead!'

CHAPTER NINE

IT WAS dusk when Ross and Vivien finally turned from the highway on to a private road. Narrow and dusty, it wound a slow, steady route through flat, almost grassless fields where Vivien only spotted one small flock of sheep, but she declined asking where the rest of the stock was. She wouldn't have lowered herself to make conversation with the man next to her. She was still too angry with him.

How dared he threaten to practically rape her? He might not literally mean it, but she couldn't abide men who used verbal abuse and physical threats to intimidate women. It just showed you the sort of man Ross was underneath his surface charm. As for suggesting that she would actually enjoy it...

That galled most of all. Because she wasn't at all sure that she *wouldn't*!

Self-disgust kept her temper simmering away in a grimly held silence while she stared out of the passenger window, her lips pressed angrily together. Eventually, the flat paddocks gave way to rolling brown hills. One was quite steep, and, as they came over the crest, there, in the distance, lay some bluish-looking mountains. But closer, on the crest of the next hill, and surrounded by tall, dark green trees, stood a home of such grandeur and elegance that Vivien caught her breath in surprise.

'I did tell you it was big,' Ross remarked drily.

'So you did,' she said equally drily, then turned flashing brown eyes his way. 'I'm allowed to talk now, am I? I won't be suitably punished for my temerity in opening my blood-red lips?'

His sigh was weary. It made Vivien suddenly feel small. What was the matter with her? She was rarely reduced to using such vicious sarcasm. She could be stubborn, but usually quietly so, with a cool, steely determination that was far more effective than more volatile methods. Yet here she was, flying off the handle at every turn. Snapping and snarling like a she-cat.

It had to be her hormones, she decided unhappily. God, but she was a mess!

She turned to look once more at the huge house, and as they drew closer an oddly apprehensive shiver trickled down her spine. Vivien knew immediately that she would not like living at Mountainview. If she stayed the full month, she would be very surprised. Yet she could not deny it was a beautiful-looking home. Very beautiful indeed.

Edwardian in style and two-storeyed, with long, graceful white columns running from the stone-flagged patio right up through the upper-floor wooden veranda to the gabled roof. An equally elegant white ironwork spanned the distance between these columns, for decoration alone downstairs, but for safety as well between the bases of the upstairs pillars.

Not that Vivien could picture too many youngsters climbing over that particular railing anyway. The house had a museum-like quality about it, enhanced possibly by the fact that only a couple of lights shone in the windows as they drove up in the rapidly fading light.

The Range Rover crunched to a halt on the gravel driveway, Ross turning to Vivien with an expectant look on his face. 'Well? What do you think of it?'

'It's—er—very big.'

'You don't like it,' he said with amazement in his voice and face.

'No, no,' she lied. 'It's quite spectacular. I'm just very tired, Ross.'

His face softened and Vivien turned hers away. She wished he didn't have the capacity to look at her like that, with such sudden warmth and compassion. It turned her bones to water, making her feel weak and vulnerable. Instinct warned her that Ross was not a man you showed such a vulnerability to.

'You must be,' he said as he opened his door. 'I'll take you inside then come back for the luggage. Once you're settled in the kitchen with one of Helga's mugs of tea you'll feel better.'

It was only after she alighted that Vivien recognised the truth of her excuse to Ross. Yet she was more than tired. She was exhausted. Her legs felt very heavy and she had to push them to lug her weary body up the wide, flagged steps. When she hesitated on the top step, swaying slightly, Ross's hand shot out to steady her.

'Are you all right, Vivien?'

She took a couple of deep breaths. 'Yes, I think so. Just a touch dizzy there for a sec.'

Before she could say another word he swept one arm around her waist, the other around her knees, and hoisted her up high into his arms. 'I'll carry you straight up to bed. Helga can bring your tea to your room. You can meet Dad in the morning.'

Suddenly, Vivien felt too drained to protest. She went quite limp in Ross's arms, her head sagging against his chest, her hands linking weakly around his neck lest they flop down by her sides like dead weights. Her eyelashes fluttered down to rest on the darkly smudged shadows beneath her eyes. She felt rather than saw Ross's careful ascent up a long flight of stairs.

'You're very strong,' she whispered once in her semiconscious daze.

He didn't answer.

Next thing she knew she was being lowered on to a soft mattress, her head sinking into a downy pillow. She felt her sandals being pulled off, a rug or blanket being draped over her legs. She sighed a shuddering sigh as the last of her energy fled her body. Within sixty seconds she was fast asleep, totally unaware of the man standing beside the bed staring down at her with a tight, pained look on his face.

After an interminable time, he bent to lightly touch her cheek, then to draw a wisp of hair from where it lay across her softly parted lips. His hand lingered, giving in to the urge to rub gently against the pouting flesh. She stirred, made a mewing sound like a sleepy kitten that had been dragged from its mother's teat. Her tongue-tip flicked out to moisten dry lips, the action sending a spurt of desire to his loins so sharp that he groaned aloud.

Spinning on his heels, he strode angrily from the room.

Vivien woke to the sound of raised voices. For a moment she couldn't remember where she was, or whose voices they could possibly be. But gradually her eyes and brain refocused on where she was.

Once properly awake, one quick glance took in the large, darkly furnished bedroom, the double bed she was lying on, the moonlight streaming in the open french doors on to the polished wooden floors, the balcony beyond those doors. Levering herself up on to one elbow, she noticed that on the nearest bedside table rested a tray, which held a tall glass of milk and a plate on which was a sandwich, a piece of iced fruit cake and a couple of plain milk-coffee biscuits.

But neither the room nor the food was of any real interest to Vivien at that moment. Her whole attention was on the argument that was cutting through the still night air with crystal clarity.

'I don't understand why you had to bring her here,' a male voice snarled. 'How do you think Becky's going to feel when she finds out? You've broken her heart, do you know that? I was over there today and she—'

'What do you mean, you were over there today?' Ross broke in testily. 'You were supposed to be checking all the bores today.'

'Yeah, well, I didn't, did I? I'll do them tomorrow.'

'Tomorrow... You've always got some excuse, haven't you? God, Gavin, when are you going to learn some sense of responsibility? Don't you know that one day without water could be the difference between life and death in a drought like this? What on earth's the matter with you? Why don't you grow up?'

'I *am* grown-up. And I *can* be responsible. It's just that you and Dad won't give me a chance at any real responsibility. All you give me is orders!'

'Which you can't follow.'

'I can too.'

'No you bloody well can't! Just look at the bores to-day.'

'Oh, bugger the bores. We've hardly got any sheep left anyway. You sold them all.'

'Better sold than dead.'

'That was your opinion. You never asked me for mine. I would have kept them, hand-fed them.'

'At what cost? Be sensible, Gavin. I made the right business decision, the only decision.'

'Business! Since when has life on the land been reduced to nothing but business decisions? Since *you* came home to run things, that's when. You're a hard-hearted ruthless bastard, Ross, who'll stop at nothing to get what you want. And I know what that is. You want Mountainview. The land and the house. Not just your half, either. You want it all! That's why you were going to marry Becky. Not because you fell in love with her, but because you knew Dad was keen for one of us to marry and produce an heir before he died. That's why you dumped Becky and brought that other city bitch back here. Because she's already having your kid. You think that will sway Dad into changing his will all the sooner. Yeah, now I see it. I see it all!'

'You're crazy,' Ross snapped. 'Or crazy drunk. Is that it? Have you been drinking again?'

'So what if I have?'

'I should have known. You're only this irrational—and this articulate—when you're drunk.'

'Not like you, eh, big brother? You've got the gift of the gab all the time, haven't you? You can charm the birds right out of the trees. I'll bet that poor bitch upstairs doesn't even know what part she's playing in all this.

You've got it made, haven't you? The heir you needed plus a hot little number on tap. A lay, laid on every night. I'll bet she's good in bed too. I'll bet she—'

The sounds of a scuffle replaced the voices. Vivien sat bolt upright, her heart going at fifty to the dozen, her mind whirling with all sorts of shocking thoughts. Could Gavin really be right? Was she some pawn in a game much larger and darker than she'd ever imagined? Were she and her child to be Ross's ace card in gaining the inheritance his brother seemed to think he coveted? It would explain why Ross had not made love to this Becky if he didn't really love her...

Shakily, she stood up and made her way out on to the balcony. The night air was silent now, the earlier sounds of fighting having stopped. The sky overhead was black and clear with a myriad stars, the moon a bright orb, bathing everything beneath in its pale, ghostly light.

Gingerly, Vivien looked down over the railing.

Ross was standing there on the driveway next to his Range Rover, disconsolate and alone. While she watched silently, he lifted his hands to rake back his dishevelled hair, expelling a ragged sigh. 'Crazy fool,' he muttered.

Vivien didn't think she made a move, or a sound. But suddenly Ross's head jerked up and those piercing eyes were staring straight into hers. Worried first, then assessing, he held her startled gaze for several seconds before speaking. And then it was to say only three sharp words, 'Stay right there.'

She barely had time to compose her rattled self before Ross was standing right in front of her, his big strong hands gripping her upper arms, his sharp blue eyes boring down into hers.

'How much did you hear?' he demanded to know.

'E—e-enough,' she stammered.

'Enough. Dear God in heaven. And did you believe what that fool said? *Did* you?' he repeated, shaking her.

Vivien could hardly think. 'I…I don't know what to believe any more.'

'*Don't* believe what my brother said, for Pete's sake,' Ross insisted harshly. 'He's all mixed up in the head at the moment. Believe what *I* tell you, Vivien. Your presence here has nothing to do with Mountainview. Nothing at all! You're here only because I want you here, because I…I… Goddammit, woman, why do you have to be so darned beautiful?'

And, digging his fingers into her flesh, he lifted her body and mouth to his, taking it wildly and hungrily in a savage kiss. For a few tempestuous moments, she found herself responding to his desperate desire, parting her lips and allowing his tongue full reign within her mouth. But when he groaned and swept his arms down around her, pressing the entire length of her against him, the stark evidence of a full-blooded male erection lying between them slammed her back to reality.

'No!' she gasped, wrenching her mouth from his. 'Let me go!' With a tortured cry, she struggled free of his torrid embrace, staggering back against the railing, staring up at him with wide, accusing eyes.

'You…you said this wasn't why you brought me here,' she flung at him shakily. 'You promised to keep your hands off.'

The sudden and shocking suspicion that he might have been using sex to direct her mind away from Gavin's accusations blasted into Vivien's brain, making her catch her breath. Dear heaven, he couldn't be that wicked, could he? Or that devious?

She stared at Ross, trying to find some reassurance now in his flushed face and heaving chest, as well as the memory of his explicit arousal. That, at least, was not a sham, she conceded. That was real. *Too* real.

But then his desire for her had always been real. That did not mean Gavin wasn't telling the truth. Ross could still be the ruthless opportunist his brother accused him of being, one who could quite happily satisfy his lust for her while achieving his own dark ends.

'I promised there would not be a repeat of what happened that night at Wallaby Creek,' he ground out. 'And there won't.'

'And...and what was that you were just doing if not trying to seduce me?' she blustered, still not convinced, despite his sounding amazingly sincere.

'That was my being a bloody idiot. But I was only kissing you, Vivien. Don't hang me for a simple kiss. Still, I will endeavour to keep my hands well and truly off in future. As for my reasons for bringing you here...I can only repeat it has everything to do with my child, but nothing to do with Mountainview. You have my solemn oath on that. Now go back to bed. You still look tired. I'll see you in the morning.'

Vivien stared after him as he whirled and strode off along the balcony and around the corner.

A simple kiss? There'd been nothing simple about that kiss. Nothing simple at all...

And there was nothing simple about this whole situation.

Though had there ever been?

Vivien lifted trembling hands to push the hair back off her face. God knew where all this was going to end. Perhaps it would be best if she cut her visit short here, if she declined taking the position as companion to Ross's father. There were too many undercurrents going on in this household, too many mysteries, too much ill feeling.

Vivien wanted no part in them. Life was complicated enough without getting involved in family feuds. Yes, she would tell Ross in the morning that she wanted to go back home.

Feeling marginally better, Vivien made her way back into the bedroom, intending to drink the milk then change into some nightwear before going back to bed. But she found herself lying down again, fully dressed, on top of the bed. Soon, she was sound asleep again.

CHAPTER TEN

WHEN Vivien woke a second time, it was morning. Mid-morning, by the feel of the heat already building in the closed room. Her slim silver wristwatch confirmed her guess. It was ten-fifteen.

With a groan she swung her stiffened legs over the side of the bed and sat up, thinking to herself that she could do with a shower. It was then that she remembered her decision of the night before to go straight back home.

Somehow, however, in the clear light of day, that seemed a hasty, melodramatic decision. She'd been very tired last night. Overwrought, even. Perhaps she should give Ross and his father and Mountainview a few days at least.

As for Gavin's accusations that his older brother was a ruthless bastard intent on using Vivien and her baby to gain an inheritance... Well, that too felt melodramatic, now that she could think clearly. Ross might be a typically selfish male in some ways, but she had sensed nothing from him but true affection and concern for his family. She'd also been impressed by the way he'd handled things with *her* parents. Ross was not a cruel, callous man. Not at all.

Yes. The matter was settled. She would stay a while. A week, at least. Then, if things weren't working out, she would make some excuse and go home. She could always say she couldn't stand the heat. That would hardly be a lie, Vivien thought, as beads of perspiration started trickling down between her breasts.

Feeling the call of nature, she rose and went to investigate the two panelled wooden doors that led off the bedroom. The first was an exit, leading out on to a huge rectangular gallery. The second revealed an *en suite* that, though its décor was in keeping with the house's Edwardian style, was still obviously fairly new.

Vivien was amused by the gold chain she had to pull to flush the toilet, smiling as she washed her hands with a tiny, shell-like soap.

On going back into the hot room, she started unpacking, having spied her suitcase resting on the ottoman at the foot of the bed. A shower was definitely called for, she decided, plus nothing heavier to wear than shorts and a cool top.

Since everything was very crushed she chose a simple shorts set in a peacock-blue T-shirt material, with a tropical print of yellow and orange hibiscus on it. The creases would fall out if she hung it up behind the bathroom door while she had a shower. With the outfit draped over an arm, and some fresh underwear and her bag of toiletries filling both hands, Vivien made for the shower.

The hot water felt so delicious that she wallowed in it for ages, shampooing her hair a couple of times during the process, the heat having made her thick black tresses feel limp and greasy. Once clean, however, her hair sprang around her face and shoulders in a myriad damp curls and waves. In deference to the heat, Vivien bypassed full make-up, putting on a dab of coral lipstick, a minimal amount of waterproof mascara and a liberal lashing of Loulou, her favourite perfume.

Electing to leave her hair damp rather than blow-dry it, Vivien opened the door of the bathroom feeling refreshed but a little nervous. What was she supposed to do? Where should she go?

The unexpected sight of a large grey-haired woman in a mauve floral dress bustling to and fro across the bedroom, hanging Vivien's clothes up for her in the elegantly carved wardrobe, replaced any nerves with a stab of surprise. And a degree of dry amusement.

So this was Helga...

'And good morning to you too,' Helga threw across the room before she could say a word. 'High time you got up. Nothing worse than lying in bed too long. Bad for the digestion. I've straightened your bed and turned on the ceiling fan. Didn't you see it there? It's best to leave the windows and doors closed till the afternoon, then I'll come up and open them. We usually get an afternoon breeze. And leave your dirty washing in the linen basket in the corner.

'I'm Helga, by the way. I dare say Ross has told you about me. Not in glowing terms, I would imagine,' she added with a dry cackle. 'We never did get along, me and that lad. He's not the sort to follow orders kindly. Still, he's turned out all right, I guess. Loves his dad, which goes down a long way with me.'

She drew breath at last to give Vivien the once-over. 'Well, you certainly are one stunning-looking girl, aren't you? But then, I wouldn't expect any different from Ross. Only the best would ever do for him. Fancy schools in Sydney. Fancy flying lessons. Now a fancy woman...'

Vivien drew in a sharply offended breath, and was just about to launch into a counter-attack when Helga dismissed any defensive speech with a sharp wave of her hand.

'Now don't go getting your knickers all in a knot, lovie. No offence intended. Besides, there's no one happier than me that you put a spoke in Ross's plans to marry Becky. I presume you know who Becky is?'

Vivien found herself nodding dumbly. She'd never met anyone quite like Helga. Talk about intimidating! Ross had her undying admiration if he stood up to this bull-dozer of a woman.

'Well, let me tell you a little secret about Miss Becky Macintosh,' Helga boomed on. 'She's always hankered after living at Mountainview, ever since she was knee-high to a grasshopper. She's no more in love with Ross than I am. But he's a mighty handsome man and a girl could do worse than put her slippers under his bed every night. When Oliver had his stroke and Ross came back home, Becky saw her chance and set her cap at him. Lord, butter wouldn't have melted in her mouth around him all year. But it's not the man she wants. It's Mountainview!'

Helga snapped the suitcase shut and started doing the buckles up.

'Why are you telling me all this?' Vivien asked on a puzzled note.

A sly look came over Helga's plain, almost masculine face. 'Because I don't want you worrying that you might be breaking Becky's heart if you marry Ross. That little minx will simply move on to the next brother, which will be by far the best for all concerned.'

Vivien bypassed Helga's conclusion that she wanted to marry Ross to concentrate on her next startling statement. 'You mean—'

'My Gavin loves her,' Helga broke in with a maternal passion that was unexpectedly fierce. 'He's loved her for years. But he's painfully shy around girls—unless he's been drinking. He can't seem to bring himself to tell her how he feels. Now, after this episode with Ross, he doesn't think he'll ever stand a chance. He's always felt inferior to his big brother. But if Ross moved far away…'

'I see,' Vivien murmured. 'Yes, I see…'

'You won't want to live here, will you? A city girl like you will want the bright lights. Ross likes action too, not the slowness of station life. You'll both be happy enough well away from here.'

Looking at Helga's anxious face, Vivien was moved to pity for her. She must love Gavin very, very much. As for Gavin… Her heart really went out to him. It couldn't be easy being Ross's brother. Even harder with the two brothers loving the same girl. That was one factor Helga had blithely forgotten. What of Ross's feelings in all this? Or didn't they count?

'I'm sorry, Helga,' she explained, 'but Ross and I have no plans to marry. We're not in love, you see.'

'Not in love?' Helga looked down at Vivien's stomach with a disdainful glower. 'Then what are you doing having his child? Not in love! Well, I never! What's the world coming to, I ask you, with girls going round having babies with men they don't love? It makes one ashamed of one's own sex!'

Vivien's lovely brown eyes flashed defiance as she drew herself up straight and proud.

'I would think you should feel more ashamed of this Becky than me,' she countered vehemently. 'At least I'm honest about my feelings. She sounds like a shallow, ma-

terialistic, manipulative little witch, and I'm not sorry at
all that Ross is not going to marry her. He deserves better
than that. Much better. He's a...a... And what are you
laughing at?' she demanded angrily when Helga started
to cackle.

Again that sly look returned. 'Just thinking what similar
personalities you and Ross have. Both as stubborn as
mules. Lord knows what kind of child you're going to
have. He'll probably end up running the world!'

'It might be a daughter!'

'Then *she'll* run the world.'

Helga grinned a highly satisfied grin, stopping Vivien
in her tracks. Against her better judgement, she found herself grinning back. She shook her head in a type of bewilderment before a sudden thought wiped the grin from
her face.

'Ross doesn't know about Gavin loving Becky, does
he?' she asked.

'No,' the older woman admitted. 'Gavin made me
promise not to tell him.'

'I see. So you told me instead, hoping I might relay the
information. That way you'd keep your promise, but get
the message across.'

Helga's look was sharp. 'There's no flies on you, lovie,
is there? Now how about a spot of breakfast? You'll want
a good plateful, I'll warrant, since you didn't eat the sup-
per I left you. Remember, you're eating for two.'

Vivien only just managed to suppress a groan of true
dismay as she slipped on her sandals and followed Helga
from the room.

The kitchen was as huge as the rest of the house. But far
more homely, with copper pots hanging over the stove,

dressers full of flowered crockery and knick-knacks lean-ing against the walls, and an enormous table in the centre.

'Do you really look after this whole place by yourself?' Vivien asked whilst Helga was piling food on to the larg-est plate she'd ever seen. She already had a mug of tea in front of her that would have satisfied a giant.

'Sure do, lovie. Keeps me fit, I can tell you. Here, get this into you!' And she slapped the plate down in front of her. There were three rashers of bacon, two eggs, a lamb chop and some grilled tomato, not to mention two slices of toast.

Vivien felt her stomach heave. Swallowing, she picked up the knife and fork and started rearranging the bacon. 'Er—do you know where Ross is this morning?' she asked by way of distraction.

'Right here,' he said, striding into the kitchen and sit-ting down in a chair opposite her. Vivien looked down, thinking that she would never get used to the way her heart skipped a beat every time she saw him. Of course, it didn't help that he only had a pair of jeans on. Not a thing on his top half. Sitting down, he looked naked.

'You look refreshed this morning, Vivien,' he said, vir-tually forcing her to look back up at him. She did, keeping her gaze well up. Unfortunately, she found herself staring straight at his mouth and remembering how she had felt when he'd kissed her last night.

'I presume you want a mug of tea?' Helga asked Ross.

'Sure do. And a piece of that great Christmas cake you made.'

Helga threw him a dry look. 'No need to suck up to

me, my lad. Your girl and I are already firm friends, aren't we, lovie?'

'Oh—er—yes,' Vivien stammered, which brought a surprised look from Ross.

'I see she appreciates your cooking as well,' he said, and gave Vivien a sneaky wink. She rolled her eyes at the food and he laughed. But laughter made the muscles ripple in his chest and she quickly looked down again, forcing a mouthful of egg in between suddenly dry lips.

'Where's Gavin?' Helga went on. 'Doesn't he want a cup too?'

'Nope. He's out checking bores. Won't be back till well after lunch.'

'Out checking bores?' Helga persisted. '*Today*? But it's going to be a scorcher. Why couldn't he go tomorrow?'

'Because he was supposed to have gone yesterday,' Ross informed her drily.

Helga looked pained and shook her head. 'That boy… Still, you have to understand he's been upset lately, Ross. He's not himself.'

'Well, he'd better get back to being himself quick smart,' Ross said firmly, 'or there won't be anything to do around here except have endless mugs of tea. Sheep don't live on love alone.'

A stark silence descended while Ross finished his tea and Vivien waded through as much of the huge breakfast as her stomach could stand. Finally, she pushed the plate aside, whereupon Helga frowned. Before her disapproval could erupt into words Ross was on his feet and asking Vivien if he could have a few words with her in private.

It was a testimony to Helga's formidable personality

that Vivien was grateful to be swept away into Ross's company when he was semi-naked.

'Don't let Helga bully you into eating too much,' was Ross's first comment as they walked along the hallway together.

'I'll try not to. Where...where are we going?' she asked once they moved across the tiled foyer and started up the stairs.

He slanted her a look which suggested he'd caught the nervousness behind her question and was genuinely puzzled by it. 'I need to shower and change before taking you along to meet Dad,' he explained. 'I thought we could talk at the same time.'

He stopped at the top of the stairs, his blue eyes glittering with a sardonic amusement. 'Of course, I don't expect you to accompany me into my bathroom. You can sit on my bed and talk to me from there. Let me assure you the shower is not visible from the bedroom.'

Sit on his bed...

Dear heaven, that was bad enough.

Noting that he was watching her closely, Vivien lifted her nose and adopted what she hoped was an expression of utter indifference. 'I doubt it would bother me if it was,' she repudiated. 'I've seen it all before.'

His features tightened, but he said nothing, ushering her along the upstairs hall and into his bedroom, shutting the door carefully behind them. When he saw her startled look, a wry smile lifted the grimness from his face.

'You may be blasé about male nudity, Vivien, my dear, but Helga is not so sophisticated. Do sit down, however. You make me uncomfortable standing there with your hands clasped defensively in front of you. I had no dark or dastardly plan in bringing you up here, though I appreciate now that my idea of having a normal chat with you while I showered was stupid. Best I simply hurry with my ablutions and then we'll talk.'

Five minutes later he came out of the closed bathroom dressed in bright shorts and a loose white T-shirt with a colourful geometric design on the back and a surfing logo on the sleeves.

It was the longest five minutes Vivien had ever spent. Who would have believed the sound of a shower running could be so disturbing?

'You look as if you're ready to shoot the waves at Bondi,' she commented, mocking herself silently for the way she was openly feasting her eyes on him this time. But she couldn't seem to help herself.

'Dad likes bright clothes. They cheer him up.'

'That's good,' she said, and bounced up on to her feet. 'Most of my clothes are bright.'

'So I noticed.'

'You don't approve?'

'Would it matter if I didn't?'

'No.'

His smile was dry. 'That's what I thought. Shall we go?'

'But you said you wanted to talk to me.'

'I've changed my mind. I'm sure you'll handle Dad OK. You seem to have a knack with men. Follow me.'

She did so in silence, her thoughts a-whirl. What was eating at Ross? Was it sexual frustration, or frustration of another kind? She seemed to be getting mixed messages from him. One minute she thought he admired her, though grudgingly. The next, he was openly sarcastic.

They trundled down the stairs and along a different corridor, towards the back section of the house.

'In here,' Ross directed, and opened a door into a cool, cosily furnished bed-sitting-room. She found out later that it had once been part of the servants' quarters, when Mountainview had had lots of servants. Ross had had it renovated and air-conditioned before his father came home from hospital.

'Dad?' Ross ventured softly. 'You're not asleep, are you?'

The old man resting in the armchair beside the window had had his eyes closed, his head listing to one side. But with Ross's voice his head jerked up and around, his eyes snapping open. They looked straight at Vivien, their gaze both direct and assessing.

'Hello, Mr Everton,' she said, and came forward to hold out her hand. 'I'm Vivien.'

Pale, parched lips cracked back into a semblance of a smile. 'So...you're Vivien...' His eyes slid slowly down her body, then up over her shoulder towards his son. 'Now...I understand,' he said, the talking clearly an effort for him. Vivien noticed that one side of his face screwed up when he spoke, the aftermath, she realised, of his stroke. 'They don't...come along...like her...too often...'

Vivien was slightly put out by his remarks. Why did men have to reduce women to sex objects?

'They don't come along like Ross too often either,' she countered, quite tartly.

The old man laughed, and immediately was consumed by racking coughs. Ross raced to pick up the glass of water resting on the table beside him, holding him gently around the shoulders till the coughing subsided, then pressing the water to his lips. Vivien hovered, feeling use-less and a little guilty. She should have kept her stupid, proud mouth shut! The man meant no harm.

'You should let me call in the doctor, Dad,' Ross was saying worriedly. 'This coughing of yours is getting worse.'

'No...more...doctors,' his father managed to get out. 'No more. They'll only...put me...in hospital. I want to...to die here.'

Ross's laugh was cajoling. 'You're not going to die, Dad. Dr Harmon said that with a little more rest and ther-apy you'll be as good as new.'

'Perhaps,' he muttered. 'Perhaps. Now...get lost. I wish...to talk...to Vivien. *Alone*. You cramp...my style.'

'All right. But don't talk too much, mind?' And Ross lanced his father with an oddly sharp look. 'You'll find me in the library when he's finished with you, Vivien.'

'Call me...Oliver,' was the first thing Ross's father said once they were alone. 'Now, tell me...all about... yourself.'

For over an hour, Vivien chatted away, answering Oliver's never-ending questions. It worried her that he was becoming overtired, but every time she touched on the subject of his health he vetoed her impatiently.

It was clear where Ross had got his determination and stubbornness. Yet, for all his questions, Oliver never once enquired about her feelings for his son, or Ross's for her. He never asked her what she wanted for the future, either for herself or her baby. He wanted to know about her background, her growing-up years, her education, her job and her family. Finally, he sighed and leant back into the chair.

'You'll do, Vivien,' he said. 'You'll do...'

'As what, Oliver?'

His smile was as cunning as Helga's. 'Why...as the mother...of my grandchild. What else? Now run along... It's lunchtime... But tell Ross...I don't want...any.'

Vivien closed the door softly, her mind still on Ross's father.

Oliver Everton didn't fool her for one minute. He was going to try to marry her off to Ross. Not that she blamed him. Death was very definitely knocking at his door and he wanted things all tied up with pink bows before he left this world.

Gavin was accusing the wrong man when he said Ross was trying to manipulate his father. It was the father who was the manipulator, who had perhaps always been the manipulator at Mountainview. Maybe that was why Ross had chosen to follow a career away from home, and why Gavin hadn't. The stronger brother bucking the heavy hand of the father while the weaker one knuckled under.

Now, illness had brought the prodigal—and perhaps favoured—son home and the father was going to make the most of it. Vivien wouldn't put it past Oliver having been the one to insist Ross bring her out here, hoping that the sexual attraction that had once flared out of control between them would do so again, thereby making his job easier of convincing them marriage was the best course for all concerned.

And he'd been half right, the cunning old devil. That electric chemistry was still sparking as strong as ever. She could hardly look at Ross without thinking about that night, without longing to find out if the wonder of it all had been real or an illusion. How long, she worried anew, before her own body language started sending out those tell-tale waves of desire in Ross's direction? How long before his male antennae picked up on them?

He was not a man to keep promises he sensed she didn't want him to keep. He was a sexual predator, a hunter. He would zero in for the kill the moment she weakened. Of that she was certain.

So why stay? her conscience berated. Why tempt fate?

Because she had to. For some reason she just had to...

CHAPTER ELEVEN

'THERE you are!' Vivien exclaimed exasperatedly when she finally found the library. 'This house is like a maze.'

'Only downstairs,' Ross said, having glanced up from where he was sitting behind a large cedar desk in the far corner. With her arrival, he put the paperwork he was doing in a drawer and stood up. 'You must have really got along with Dad to stay so long.'

'Yes, I did,' she agreed, glancing around the room, which was exactly as she'd first imagined. Leather furniture, heavy velvet curtains and floor-to-ceiling bookshelves. 'I think he quite likes me.'

'I don't doubt it,' Ross muttered as he strode round the desk, his caustic tone drawing both her attention and her anger.

'Do you *have* to be sarcastic all the time?'

'Am I?' There was an oddly surprised note in his voice, as though he hadn't realised his bad manners.

'Yes, you are!'

'You're exaggerating, surely. I think I've been very polite, in the circumstances. Well? What did you think of Dad?'

Vivien sighed her irritation at having her complaint summarily brushed aside. What circumstances did he mean, anyway?

'He's a very sick man,' she commented at last.

'He's as strong as an ox,' came the impatient rebuttal.

'Not any longer, Ross. Maybe you've been away from home too long.'

'Meaning?'

She shrugged. 'People change. Things change.'

'I get the impression I'm supposed to read between the lines here.' Ross leant back against the corner of the desk, his arms folding. 'What's changed around Mountainview that I don't know about?'

Vivien frowned. This was not going to be easy, but it had to be done. 'Well, for one thing...did you know Gavin was in love with Becky?'

Ross straightened, his face showing true shock. 'Good God, he isn't, is he?'

She nodded slowly.

'Who told you that? It couldn't have been Dad!'

'No. Helga.'

He groaned, his shoulders sagging. 'Bloody hell. Poor Gavin...'

'Helga also says Becky doesn't really love you. She says the girl has always coveted Mountainview.'

Ross's eyes jerked up, angry this time. 'Damn and blast, what is this? You've been in this house less than twenty-four hours and already you know more about what's going on around here than I do. Why hasn't someone told me any of this? Why tell you? What do you have that I don't have?'

She looked past his anger, fully understanding his resentment. 'Objectivity, perhaps?' she tried ruefully.

'Objectivity?' His lips curled into a snarl. 'Oh, yes, you've got that all right, haven't you?'

She wasn't quite sure what he meant by that. Maybe

he didn't mean anything. Maybe he just felt the need to lash out blindly. 'Ross, I...I'm really sorry.'

'For what?'

'For being the one to tell you that the woman you're in love with doesn't love you back.'

He stared at her, his blue eyes icy with bitterness. 'You don't have to be sorry about that, Vivien,' he bit out coldly. 'Because I already knew that. I've known it all along.'

'But...but—'

'You of all people should know that love is not always returned. But that doesn't stop you from loving that person, does it? Aren't you still in love with your Earl?'

'I...I'm not sure...'

'Real love doesn't cease as quickly as that, my dear,' he scorned. 'You either loved the man or you didn't. What was it?'

'I *did* love him,' she insisted, hating the feeling of being backed into a corner. But if he expected her to admit to not loving a man she'd lived with for nearly eighteen months then he was heartily mistaken. Yet even as she made the claim she knew it to be a lie. She had not loved Earl. Not really.

'Then you still do,' he insisted fiercely. 'Believe me. You still do. Now I must go and talk to my father. If what you say is all true then I have no time to waste. Things have to be done before it's too late.'

'Too late for what? What things?'

His returning look was cool. 'That is not your concern. You've done your objective duty. Now I suggest you go and have some lunch, then do what pregnant ladies do on a hot afternoon. Lie down and rest. Or, if that doesn't appeal, read one of these books. I'm sure there's enough of a selection here to satisfy the most catholic of tastes.'

'Ross!' she called out as he went to leave.

He turned slowly, his face hard.

'Please...don't be angry with me...'

The steely set to his mouth softened. He sighed. 'I'm not. Not really...'

'You...you seem to be.'

The slightest of smiles touched his mouth, but not his eyes. 'It's fate I'm angry with, Vivien. Fate...'

'Now you're being cryptic.'

'Am I? Yes, possibly I am. Let's say then that I'm angry with what I have no control over.'

'But you're not angry with me personally.'

'No.'

'Then will you show me around the house later, after you're finished with your father?'

He stared at her for a moment, his eyes searching. 'It will be my pleasure,' he said with a somewhat stiff little bow.

'I...I'll probably be here,' she said. 'I don't want any lunch. Oh, that reminds me. Your father said to tell you he didn't want any lunch either.'

A dry smile pulled at Ross's mouth. 'Helga *will* be pleased.' And, giving her one last incisive and rather disturbing glance, he turned and left the room.

Vivien stared after him, aware that her heart was pounding. Already, she was looking forward to his return, knowing full well that it wasn't the thought of a tour through this house that was exciting her. It was the prospect of being alone again with Ross.

A shiver ran through her. Oh, Oliver...you are a wicked, wicked man.

Ross returned shortly after two to find Vivien curled up in one of the large lounge chairs, trying valiantly to read a copy of *Penmarric*. The book was probably as good as everyone had told her it was, but she just hadn't been able to keep her mind on it.

Once the reason for this walked into the room she abandoned all pretence at finding the book engrossing, snapping it shut with an almost relieved sigh.

'Finished your business?' she said, and uncurled her long legs.

'For now. Come on, if you want to see the house.'

His tone was clipped, his expression harried. Clearly, his visit to his father had not been a pleasant one. Vivien wished she could ask him what it was all about, but Ross's closed face forbade any such quizzing. Instead, she put the book back and went to join him in the doorway, determined to act as naturally as possible.

But her resolve to ignore the physical effect Ross kept having on her was waylaid when he moved left just as she moved right and they collided midstream. His hands automatically grabbed her shoulders and suddenly there they were, chest to chest, thigh to thigh, looking into each other's eyes.

Vivien gave a nervous laugh. 'Sorry.'

Ross said absolutely nothing. But there was no doubting he was as agitated by her closeness as she was by his. After what felt like an interminable delay, his hands dropped from her shoulders and he stepped back. 'After you,' he said with a deep wave of his right hand and a self-mocking look on his face. See? it said. I'm a man of my word. I'm keeping my hands off.

But did Vivien want him to keep his hands off? So much had changed now. Becky didn't love him, and, while Ross might think he loved her, there was no doubting he was still very attracted to *herself*. And what of her own feelings for Ross? Had they changed too? Deepened, maybe?

She couldn't be sure, certainly not with the chemistry between them still sparking away at a million volts. Vivien would just have to wait a while longer to find out about her feelings. That was what her mother had told her to do. Wait.

'Oh, my God, *Mum*!' she gasped aloud.

Ross looked taken aback. 'What about her?'

'I forgot to ring her, let her know we arrived all right. She'll be worried to death, and so will Dad.'

'Worried?' His smile carried a wry amusement. 'About their highly independent, very sensible, grown-up girl?'

'Who happens to be on her way to being an unmarried mother,' was her droll return. 'That's really surpassing myself in common sense, isn't it? Now point me to a telephone, Ross, or you'll have my mother on your doorstep.'

'There's an extension in the foyer, underneath the stairs.'

Unfortunately, Ross sat on those stairs while she dialled the number, making her feel self-conscious about what she was going to say. The phone at the other end only rang once before it was swept up.

'Peggy Roberts here,' her mother answered in a breathless tone.

'Mum, it's Vivien.'

'Oh, Vivien, darling! I'm so glad you rang. I've been rather worried.'

'No need, Mum. I'm fine. Sorry I didn't ring sooner, but by the time we arrived last night I was so tired I went straight to bed and slept in atrociously late this morning. Then Ross wanted me to meet his father and we talked for simply ages.'

'Oh? And how is Mr Everton senior? Getting better, I hope.'

'Well, he—er—reminded me a little of Uncle Jack a few weeks after his stroke.'

'You mean just before he died?'

'Er—yes…'

'Oh, dear. Oh, how sad. Well, be nice to him, dear. And be nice to Ross. He's a sweet man, not at all what your father and I were expecting. We were very impressed with him.'

'So I noticed.'

'You don't think that you and he—er—might…' She left the words hanging. *Get married*?

Vivien knew what would happen if she even hinted marriage was vaguely possible. She'd never hear the end of it. Yet her mother's even asking the question sent an odd little leap to her heart. Who knew? If Becky didn't love Ross, there might be a chance. *If* she fell in love with him, and *if* he did with her.

That was a lot of ifs.

'Not at this stage, Mum.'

'Oh…' Disappointment in her voice.

'Give Dad my love and tell him not to worry about me. I know he worries.'

'We both do, dear. Do you know how long you'll be staying out there?' Now her voice was wistful.

'Can't say. I'll write. Tell you all about the place. Must fly. I don't like to stay on someone else's phone too long.'

'I'll write to you too.'

'Yes, please do. Bye, Mum. Keep well.'

'Bye, darling. Thanks for ringing.'

Swallowing, she replaced the receiver and walked round to the foot of the stairs. Ross was sitting a half-dozen steps up, looking rather like a lost little boy. Suddenly, Vivien thought of *his* mother. What had she been like? Did he still miss her? She knew she would die if anything happened to her mother. Much as Peggy sometimes interfered and fussed, Vivien always knew the interference and fuss was based on the deepest of loves, that of a mother for her child.

Automatically, she thought of her own baby, and a soft smile lit her face. For the first time, she felt really positive about her decision to have Ross's baby. No matter what happened, that part was right. Very right indeed.

'You look very pleased with yourself,' he remarked as he stood up. 'Anything I should know about?'

'No,' she said airily. 'Not really. Mum's fine. Dad's fine. Everything's fine.'

His eyes narrowed suspiciously. 'You look like the cat who's discovered a bowl of cream.'

Her laugh was light and carefree. 'Do I?'

'You also look incredibly beautiful...'

Her eyes widened when he started walking down the stairs towards her. Perhaps he interpreted her reaction for alarm for his expression quickly changed to one of exasperation. 'No need to panic, Vivien. I'm not about to pounce. I was merely stating a fact. You know, you look somewhat like my mother when she was young. No wonder Dad took to you.'

Vivien did her best to cool the rapid heating Ross's compliments had brought to her blood, concentrating instead on the opening he'd just given her. 'How odd,' she commented. 'I was just thinking about your mother, wondering what she was like.'

'Were you? That *is* odd. What made you think of her?'

'You wouldn't want to know,' she chuckled.

'Wouldn't I?'

'No,' she said firmly, and, linking her arm with his, turned him to face across the foyer. 'So come on, show me your house and tell me about your mother.'

Ross stared down at her for a second before moving. 'To what do I owe this new Vivien?' he asked warily.

'This isn't a new Vivien. This is the real me.'

'Which is?'

She grinned. 'Charming. Witty. Warm.'

'What happened to stubborn, infuriating and uncooperative?'

'I left them in Sydney.'

'You could have fooled me.'

'Apparently I have.'

'Vivien, I—'

'Oh, do stop being so serious for once, Ross,' she cut in impatiently. 'Life's too short for eternal pessimism.'

'It's also too short for naïve optimism,' he muttered.

His dark mood refused to lift, especially when he saw Vivien's reaction to the house. But she found it difficult to pretend real liking for the place. She favoured open, airy homes with lots of light and glass and modern furniture, not dark rooms surrounded by busy wallpaper and crammed to the rafters with heavy antiques. Still, she could see why a person of another mind might covet the place. It had to be worth heaps.

'You definitely do not like this house,' Ross announced as they traipsed upstairs.

'Well, it's not exactly my taste,' Vivien admitted at last. 'Sorry.'

'You don't have to apologise.'

'I like the upstairs better. There's more natural light in the rooms.'

The floor plan was simpler too, all the rooms coming off the central gallery and all opening out on to the upstairs veranda. There were ten bedrooms, five with matching *en suites* and five without. Any guests using the latter shared the two general bathrooms, Ross informed her. Finally, Vivien was shown the upstairs linen-room, which was larger than her mother's bedroom back home.

'My mother,' Ross explained, 'had an obsession for beautiful towels and sheets.'

Vivien could only agree as her disbelieving eyes encompassed the amount of Manchester goods on the built-in shelves. There was enough to stock a whole section in a department store.

'To tell the truth,' he went on, 'I don't think Mum liked this house any more than you do. Or maybe it was the land she didn't like. She was city, just like you.'

'Really?'

'Yes, really. Well, that's about it, Vivien,' he said as he ushered her out of the linen-room and locked the door. 'I must leave you now. I have to check on Gavin's progress with the bores. Perhaps you should have a rest this afternoon. You're looking hot. Dinner is at seven-thirty when we have visitors, and, while not formal, women usually wear a dress. I dare say I'll see you then. *Au revoir...*' And, tipping his forehead, he turned and strode away, his abrupt departure leaving her feeling empty and quite desolate.

Vivien shook her head, wishing she could come to grips with what she felt for this man. Was it still just sex? Or had it finally become more complicated than that?

There was one way to find out, came the insidious temptation. Let him make love to you again. See if the fires can be burn out. See if there is anything else left after the night is over...

Vivien trembled. Did she have the courage to undertake such a daring experiment. Did she?

Yes, she decided with unexpected boldness, a shudder of sheer excitement reverberating through her. Yes. She did!

But no sooner had the scandalous decision been made than the doubts and fears crowded in.

What if she made a fool of herself? What if her second time with Ross proved to be an anticlimax? What if—oh, lord, was it possible?—what if Ross *rejected* her?

No, she dismissed immediately. He wouldn't do that. Not if she offered herself to him on a silver platter. He'd admitted once he'd found her sexually irresistible. He wouldn't knock back a night of free, uncomplicated loving in her bed.

And that was what she was going to offer him.

There were to be no strings attached. No demands. No extracted promises. Just a night of sex.

Vivien shuddered with distaste. How awful that sounded. How…cheap.

Yet she was determined not to go back on her decision, however much her conscience balked at the crude reality of it. Life was full of crude realities, she decided with some bitterness. Earl had been one big crude reality. He'd made her face the fact that sex and love did not always go together. Now Vivien was determined to find out if her feelings for Ross were no more than what Earl had felt for her, or whether they had deepened to something potentially more lasting.

Maybe she wouldn't have been so desperate to find out if she weren't expecting Ross's baby. But she was, and, if there was some chance of having a real relationship with her baby's father, one that could lead to marriage, then she was going to go for it, all guns blazing. Married parents were a darned sight better for a baby's upbringing than two single ones.

Thinking about her baby's welfare gave Vivien the inner strength to push any lingering scruples aside. For the first time in weeks, she felt as if she was taking control of her life, making her own decisions for the future. And it felt good. Surprisingly good. She hadn't realised how much of her self-confidence had been undermined by what Earl had done to her. Losing her job hadn't helped either.

So it was with an iron determination that Vivien returned to her bedroom and set to pondering how one successfully seduced a man.

The practicalities of it weren't as easy as one might have imagined. She'd never had to seduce a man in her life before. Earl had made the first move. So had Ross. Neither was she a natural flirt, except when intoxicated.

Was that the solution? she wondered. Could she perhaps have a few surreptitious drinks beforehand?

It was a thought. She would certainly keep it in mind if she felt her courage failing her.

Of course, if she dressed appropriately, maybe Ross would once again make the first move. Vivien hoped that would be the case. Now what could she wear that would turn Ross on? Something sexy, but subtle. She didn't want to look as if there was a banner on her body which read: 'Here I am, handsome. Do your stuff!'

Vivien wasn't too sure what clothes she'd brought with her. Her mother had packed most of her clothes. And Helga had unpacked them. But she was pretty sure she'd spotted her favourite black dress in there somewhere when she'd rooted around for her toiletries.

Vivien walked over and threw open the wardrobe. First she would find something to wear, then she would have a bubble bath in one of the main bathrooms and then a lie-down. She didn't want to look tired. She wanted to be as beautiful as she could be. Beautiful and desirable and *simply irresistible*.

Vivien walked slowly down the huge semi-circular staircase shortly before seven-thirty, knowing she couldn't look more enticing. The polyester-crêpe dress she was wearing was one of those little black creations that looked simple and stylish, but was very seductive.

Halter-necked, it had a bare back and shoulders, a V neckline that hinted at rather than showed too much cleavage, and a line that skimmed rather than hugged the body. With her hair piled up on to her head in studied disarray, long, dangling gold earrings at her lobes and a bucket of

Loulou wafting from her skin, a man would have had to have all his senses on hold not to find her ultra-feminine and desirable.

As Vivien put her sexily shod foot down on to the black and white tiled foyer a male voice called out to her from the gallery above.

'Wait on!'

Nerves tightened her stomach as she turned to watch Ross come down the stairs, looking very Magnumish in white trousers and a Hawaiian shirt in a red and white print. It crossed Vivien's mind incongruously that Earl would not have been seen dead in anything but a business suit.

'Don't tell me,' she said with a tinkling laugh—one she'd heard used to advantage by various vamps on television. 'You've been to Waikiki recently.'

He gave her a sharp look. Had she overdone the laugh?

'No,' he denied drily. 'This is pure Hamilton Island.'

He took the remaining few steps that separated them, icy blue eyes raking over her. 'And what is that sweet little number you've got on?' he drawled. 'Pure King's Cross?'

Vivien felt colour flood her cheeks. Had she overdone *everything*? Surely she didn't really look like a whore?

No, of course she didn't. Ross was simply being nasty for some reason. Perhaps he'd been brooding about Becky and Gavin. Or perhaps, she ventured to guess, he resented her looking sexy when he was supposed to keep his hands off.

Some instinctive feminine intuition told her this last guess was close to the mark.

Knowing any blush was well covered by her dramatic

make-up, she cocked her head slightly to one side and
slanted him a saucy look. 'Been to the Cross, have you?'

'Not lately,' he bit out, jaw obviously clenched.

'Perhaps it's time for a return visit,' she laughed. 'You
seem…tense.'

Vivien was startled when Ross's right hand shot out to
grip her upper arm, yanking her close to him. 'What in
hell's got into you tonight?' he hissed.

It was an effort to remain composed when one's heart
was pounding away like a jackhammer.

'Why does something have to have got into me?' she
returned with superb nonchalance. 'I felt like dressing up
a bit, that's all. I'm sorry you don't like the way I look,
but I won't lose any sleep over it. Now unhand me, please.
I don't take kindly to macho displays of male domination.
They always bring out the worst in me.'

Yes, she added with silent darkness. Like they make
me want to strip off all my clothes and beg you to take
me on these stairs right here and now!

'Sorry,' he muttered, and released her arm. 'I…did I
hurt you?'

'I dare say I'll have some bruises in the morning. I have
very delicate skin.'

'So I've noticed,' he ground out, his eyes igniting to
hot coals as they moved up over her bare shoulders and
down the tantalising neckline.

Vivien didn't know whether to feel pleased or alarmed
by the evidence of Ross's obvious though sneering admiration. There was something about him tonight that was
quite frightening, as though he were balancing on a razor's edge that was only partly due to male frustration.

There were other devils at work within his soul. She suspected that it wouldn't take much to tip him into violence.

'Did Gavin check all the bores?' she asked, deliberately deflecting the conversation away from her appearance and giving herself a little time to rethink the situation. Suddenly, the course of action she'd set herself upon this night seemed fraught with danger. She wanted Ross to make love to her, not assault her.

'Yes,' was his uninformative and very curt answer. He glanced at the watch on his wrist. Gold, with a brown leather band, it looked very expensive. 'Helga gets annoyed when we're late for dinner,' he pronounced. 'I think we'd better make tracks for the dining-room.'

Vivien would never have dreamt she would feel grateful for Helga's army-like sense of punctuality.

Dinner still proved a difficult meal for all concerned. Gavin, who, unlike his brother, was dressed shoddily in faded jeans and black T-shirt, was sulkily silent. This seemed to make Helga agitated and stroppy. She kept insisting everyone have seconds whether they wanted them or not.

By the time dessert came—enormous portions of plum pudding and ice-cream—Vivien's stomach was protesting. Ross, in the end, made a tactless though accurate comment to Helga about her always giving people too much to eat. Vivien managed to soothe the well-intentioned though misguided woman by saying she would normally be able to eat everything, but that her condition seemed to have affected her appetite.

At this allusion to her pregnancy, Gavin made a contemptuous sound, stood up, and stomped out of the room, having not said a word to Vivien all evening other than a grumpy hello when she and Ross had first walked into the dining-room. Shortly, they heard his station wagon start up, the gravel screeching as he roared off.

'I...I'm sorry, lovie,' Helga apologised for Gavin. 'He's not himself at the moment.'

Vivien smiled gently. 'It's all right. I understand. He's upset.'

'He's not the only one who's upset,' Ross grated out. 'I'm damned upset that people around here chose not to tell me that my own brother was in love with the girl I was going to marry.'

He glowered at Helga, who stood up with an uncompromising look on her face. 'The boy made me promise not to tell you.'

'Then why didn't he tell me himself?'

'Don't be ridiculous!' Helga snapped. 'The boy has *some* pride.'

'Haven't we all,' he muttered darkly. 'Haven't we all...'

'Anyone for tea?' Helga asked brusquely.

'Not me,' Ross returned. 'I think I'll have some port in the library instead.'

He'd asked earlier—and with some dry cynicism, Vivien had noted—if she wanted some wine with her dinner. Vivien had politely declined, whereby Ross had still opened a bottle of claret, though he'd only drunk a couple of glasses. Gavin had polished off the rest.

'What about you, lovie?'

'Er—no, thanks, Helga.' She looked over at Ross, unsure of what to do. Swallowing, she made her decision. 'I might join Ross for some port after we've cleared up,' she said in a rush.

Ross's eyes snapped round to frown at her.

'If…if that's all right with you,' she added, battling to remain calm in the face of his penetrating stare.

He lifted a single sardonic eyebrow. 'I didn't think you liked port.'

'I do occasionally.'

Actually, she *did*, though she'd only ever indulged in small quantities before. Earl had always insisted she pretend to drink at their dinner parties, saying people hated teetotallers. She'd usually managed to tip most of her wine down the sink at intervals, but she'd often allowed herself the luxury of a few sips of Earl's vintage port at the end of the evening. It seemed to relax her after the tension of cooking and serving a meal that lived up to Earl's standards.

Vivien considered she could do with some relaxing at this point in time, while she made up her mind what she was going to do. Quite clearly, Ross wasn't going to make any move towards her. Any momentary interest on the staircase appeared to have waned. He'd barely looked at her during dinner.

'I'll see you shortly, then,' Ross said, leaving the room without a backward glance.

Vivien stood up to help Helga clear the table and then wash up. They had it all finished in ten minutes flat. Never had Vivien seen anyone wash up like Helga!

'Off you go now, lovie,' the other woman said, taking the tea-towel from Vivien's hands. 'But watch yourself. Ross is stirring for a fight tonight. I've seen him like this before. He can't stand not having what he wants, or not having things go his way. Oh, he's got a good heart but he's a mighty stubborn boy. Mighty stubborn, indeed!'

Vivien was still thinking about Helga's warning when she opened the library door. So she was startled to see Ross looking totally relaxed in the large armchair she'd been sitting in earlier in the day, his feet outstretched and crossed at the ankles, a hefty glass of port cradled in his hands.

'Close the door,' he said in a soft, almost silky voice. For some reason, it brought goosebumps up on the back of her neck.

She closed the door.

'Now lock it,' he added.

She spun round, eyes blinking wide. 'Lock it? But why?'

His gaze became cold and hard. 'Because I don't like to be interrupted when I'm having sex.'

CHAPTER TWELVE

VIVIEN froze. 'I beg your pardon?'

'You heard me, Vivien. Now just lock the door and stop pretending that your sensibilities are offended. You and I both know why you dressed like that tonight. You're feeling frustrated and you've decided once again to make use of yours truly. At least, I imagine it's me you've set your cap at. I'm the one who looks like your old boyfriend, not Gavin. Or are you going to tell me you've reverted to the tease I mistook you for that night at the ball?'

Vivien's first instinct was to flee Ross's cutting contempt. For it hurt. It hurt a lot. How could she not have realised her strategy could backfire on her so badly?

But she had faced many difficult foes during her television career. Belligerent businessmen...two-faced politicians...oily con men. She was not about to let Ross's verbal attack rout her completely, though she *was* badly shaken.

'You...you've got it all wrong, Ross,' she began with as much casual confidence as she could muster.

'In what way, Vivien?'

God, but she hated that cold, cynical light in his eyes, hated the silky derision in his voice.

'I...I did try to look extra attractive tonight, but I—'

His hard, humourless laugh cut her off. '"*Extra attractive*"? Is that how you would describe yourself tonight?'

With another laugh, he uncurled his tall frame from the chair to begin moving slowly across the room like a panther stalking its prey, depositing his glass of port on a side-table on the way. Nerves and a kind of hypnotic fascination kept her silent and still while he approached. What on earth was he going to do?

Finally, he stood in front of her, tension in every line of his body.

'The dress could almost have been an unconscious mistake,' he said, smiling nastily. 'Despite the lack of underwear under it. But *not* when combined with those other wicked little touches. The hair, looking as if you'd just tumbled from a lover's bed...'

When he reached out to pull a few more tendrils around her face, she just stood there, as though paralysed.

'The earrings,' he went on, 'designed to draw attention to the sheer, exquisite delicacy of your lovely neck...'

Her mouth went dry when he trickled fingers menacingly around the base of her throat.

'The scarlet lipstick on your oh, so sexy mouth...'

Vivien almost moaned when he ran a fingertip around her softly parted lips. She squeezed her eyes tightly shut, appalled that he could make her feel like this when his touch was meant to be insulting.

But at least she was finding out the bitter truth, wasn't she? This couldn't be love—or the beginnings of love. This was raw, unadulterated sex, lust in its worst form, making her want him even while he showed his contempt. His own feelings for her were apparently similar, since he quite clearly hated wanting her nearly as much.

'Close your eyes if you like,' he jeered softly. 'I don't

mind. I've already accepted I'm to be just a proxy lover. But believe me, I'm going to enjoy you anyway.'

Her eyes flew open in angry defiance of his presumption.

'You keep away from me. I don't want you touching me!'

His answering laugh was so dark that she shrank back against the door, one hand searching blindly for the knob.

'Oh, no, you don't,' he ground out, turning the key in the lock and pocketing it before she had a hope of escaping. 'And don't bother to scream. This room is virtually sound-proof, not to mention a hell of a long way from the servants' quarters.'

She froze when he coolly reached out to undo the button at the nape of her neck, then peeled the dress down to the waist. When he ran the back of his hand across her bared breasts her head whirled with a dizzying wave of unbidden pleasure and excitement. She didn't have to look down to know that her nipples had peaked hard with instant arousal.

'Bitch,' he rasped, before suddenly pulling her to him, *crushing* her to him, his head dipping to trail a hot mouth over her shoulders and up her throat. Vivien began to tremble uncontrollably.

She moaned when he finally kissed her, knowing that there was no stopping him now, even if she wanted to.

And she *did* want to stop him. That was the irony of it all. But only with her brain. Her body, she had already found out once with Ross, could not combat the feelings he could evoke in her, the utterly mindless passion and need.

'No,' she managed once, when he abandoned her mouth briefly to kiss her throat again.

'Shut up,' was his harsh reply before taking possession of her lips again.

She felt his hands around her waist, then pushing the dress down over her hips. It pooled around her ankles with a silky whoosh. Now only a wisp of black satin and lace prevented her from being totally naked before him. It would have been a humiliating thought, if Vivien had been able to think. As it was she found herself winding her arms up around his neck and kissing him back with the kind of desperation no man could misunderstand. Her naked breasts were pressed flat against his chest, her hips moulded to his, her abdomen undulating against his escalating arousal with primitive force.

Ross groaned under the onslaught of her frantic desire, hoisting her up on to his hips and carrying her across the room, where he lay her back across the large cedar desk in the corner. The cool hardness of its smoothly polished surface brought a gasp of shock from Vivien, almost returning her to reality for a moment. But Ross didn't allow her mad passion any peace. His hands on her outstretched body kept her arousal at fever pitch till she was beside herself with wanting him.

His name fluttered from her lips on a ragged moan of desire and need.

'Yes, that's right,' he grated back with a satanic laugh while he removed the last items of clothing from her quivering body—her panties and her shoes. 'It's Ross. Not Earl. *Ross!*'

Vivien dimly reacted to his angry assertion, wondering fleetingly if he had been more deeply hurt over that Earl business than she'd imagined. But once he had access to her whole body, to that part of her that was melting for him, she forgot everything but losing herself in that erotic world of unbelievable pleasure Ross could create with his hands and lips.

'Yes…oh, yes,' she groaned when his mouth moved intimately over her heated flesh. She groaned even more when he suddenly stopped, glazed eyes flying to his.

'Say that you love me,' he demanded hoarsely as he stripped off his trousers.

A wild confusion raced through Vivien. Dazedly, she saw him smiling down at her, felt his flesh teasing hers. She didn't recognise the smile for the grimace of self-mockery it really was. All Vivien knew was that, quite unexpectedly, a raw emotion filled her heart with his demand, an emotion that both stunned and thrilled her.

'Go on,' he urged, his hands curving round her buttocks to pull her closer to the edge. And him. 'You don't have to mean it. Just say it!'

'I love you,' she whispered huskily and felt the emotion swell within her chest. The words came then, ringing with passion and truth. 'I really, truly love you, Ross.'

His groan was a groan of sheer torture. Quite abruptly, he thrust deeply into her. Vivien felt the emotion spill over into every corner of her body, felt it charging into every nerve-ending, sharpening them, electrifying them. She cried out, at the same time reaching out her arms to gather Ross close, to hold him next to her heart.

For she *did* really, truly love him. She could see it now, see it so clearly. She'd once believed Earl the real thing, and Ross just an illusion. But she had got it the wrong way round. Earl had been the illusion, Ross the real thing.

He must have fallen in love with her too, to demand such a reassurance.

So she was startled when he took her hands in an iron grip, pressing them down over the edges of the desk while he set up an oddly controlled rhythm. It was only then that she saw the ugly lines in his contorted face.

Cold, hard reality swept into her heart like a winter wind. Ross was not making love to her. He was making hate, having a kind of revenge. That was why he'd demanded she tell him she loved him. It had been nothing but a cruel parody of what she had begged of him that first night.

'Oh, God...no,' she cried out in an anguished dismay, lifting her head immediately in a valiant but futile struggle to rid herself of his flesh.

'Oh, God...yes,' he bit out and kept up his relentless surging. '*Yes!*'

She moaned in despair when she felt her body betray her, felt that excruciating tightening before her flesh shattered apart into a thousand convulsing, quivering parts. Crushingly, her climax seemed to be even more intense than anything she could remember of that night at Wallaby Creek. She almost wept with the perverse pleasure of it all, but then she felt Ross's hands tightening around hers, and he too was climaxing.

She cringed even more under his violently shuddering body. He despised her and yet he was finding the ultimate satisfaction in her body. It seemed the epitome of shame, the supreme mockery of what this act should represent.

Tears of bitter misery flooded her eyes and she began to sob.

Ross's eyes jerked up to hers as though she had struck

him. When he scooped her up to hold her hard against him, his body still blended to hers, she wanted to fight him. But every muscle and bone in her body had turned to mush.

'Leave me...be,' she sobbed. 'I...I *hate* you!'

'And I hate you,' he rasped, while keeping her weeping face cradled against his shirt-front. 'Hush, now. Stop crying. You're all right. It's just a reaction to your orgasm. It was too intense. Relax, honey. Relax...'

Vivien was amazed to find herself actually calming down under the soothing way he was stroking her back. When he moved over to sit down in the huge armchair, taking her with him, she didn't even object. Her legs were easily accommodated on either side on him, the deep cushioning allowing her knees and body to sink into a blissfully comfortable position.

Vivien even felt like going to sleep, which shocked her. She should be fighting him, hitting him, telling him he was a wicked, cruel man for doing what he had just done to her. She certainly shouldn't let him go on thinking that her pleasure had been nothing but sexual, that her crying was merely an emotional reaction to a heightened physical experience.

'You're not going to sleep, are you?' he whispered, his stroking hands coming to rest rather provocatively on her buttocks.

'No. Not quite.'

God, was that her voice? When had she ever talked in such low, husky, sexy tones?

'Tell me, Vivien,' he said thickly, 'was *any* of that for me, or is it still all for Earl?'

Vivien flinched, remembering how she'd momentarily

thought during Ross's torrid lovemaking that his resemblance to her ex-lover had affected him deeply. He certainly did keep harping on it. Why care, if it was just vengeful sex he was after? If that were the case it shouldn't matter to him whom she was thinking about.

Vivien's heart leapt. If Ross wanted her to want him for himself, and not for his likeness to Earl, then that could only be because his feelings for her were deeper than just lust. He might not realise that himself yet—she could understand his confusion with Becky still in his heart—but one day soon...

First, however, she had to convince him that Earl was dead and gone as far as she was concerned, then that might open the way to Ross letting his feelings for her rise to the surface.

She lifted heavy eyelids to look up into his face, that face which, though so like Earl's, feature for feature, no longer reminded her at all of the man who'd treated her so badly.

Her hand reached up to lie against his cheek. 'What a foolish man you are, Ross Everton,' she said tenderly. 'You are so different from Earl in so many ways. When I look at you now, I see no one else but you. It was you I was wanting today, you I dressed for tonight, you I wanted to make love to me. Not Earl...' And, stretching upwards, she pressed gentle lips to his mouth, kissing him with all the love in her heart.

He groaned, his hands lifting to cup her face, to hold it captive while he deepened her kiss into an expression of rapidly renewing desire and need. When Vivien became hotly aware of more stirring evidence of that renewing desire, her inside contracted instinctively, gripping his growing hardness with such intensity that Ross tore his mouth away from hers on a gasping groan.

'Did...did I hurt you?' she asked breathlessly, her own arousal having revved her pulse-rate up a few notches.

He laughed. 'I wouldn't put it quite like that. But perhaps you should do it again, just so I can make sure.' And, gripping her buttocks, he moved her in a slow up-and-down motion, encouraging her internal muscles to several repeat performances.

'No.' He grimaced wryly. 'That definitely does not hurt.' He stopped moving her to slide his hands up over her ribs till they found her breasts.

'Lean back,' he rasped. 'Grip the armrests.'

She did so, her heart pounding frantically as he began to play with her outstretched body, first her breasts, then her ribs and stomach, and finally between her thighs, touching her most sensitive part till she was squirming with pleasure. He seemed to like her writhing movements too, his breathing far more ragged than her own.

'Oh, yes, honey, yes,' he moaned when she started lifting her bottom up and down again, squeezing and releasing him in a wild rhythm of uninhibited loving. 'Keep going,' he urged. 'Don't stop...'

After it was all over, and they were spent once more, they did sleep, briefly, only to wake to the sound of thunder rocking the house.

'A storm,' Vivien whispered, and shivered.

'Just electrical, I suspect. There's no rain predicted. You don't like thunder?' he asked when she shivered again.

'I'm just cold.'

He held her closer if that was possible, wrapping his arms tightly around her. 'Want to go up to bed?'

'Uh-huh.'

'I'll carry you upstairs.'

'You can't carry me out of the room like this!' she exclaimed in a shocked tone.

'Why not? No one's likely to see us. Dad's sleeping-pill will have worked by now and Helga will be busily knitting in front of the television. As for Gavin…he's playing cards and drowning his sorrows with the boys down in the shearing shed. Won't be back till the wee small hours.'

'You're sure we won't run into anyone?'

'Positive.'

'If we do, I'll die of embarrassment.'

'Me too. I haven't got any trousers on, remember?'

They didn't run into anyone, despite Vivien giggling madly all the way up the stairs. They both collapsed into a shower together in Ross's *en suite*, which revived them enough to start making love all over again. This time, it was slow and erotic and infinitely more loving, the touching and kissing lasting for an hour before Ross moved over and into her. They looked deep into each other's eyes as the pleasure built and built, Ross bending to kiss her gasping mouth when she cried out in release, only then allowing himself to let go.

Vivien lay happily in his sleeping arms afterwards, feeling more at peace with herself than she had ever felt.

So this was what really being in love was like. She smiled softly to herself in the dark, pressing loving lips to the side of Ross's chest.

'And I think you love me too,' she whispered softly. 'You just don't know it yet…'

CHAPTER THIRTEEN

THREE days rolled by and Vivien was blissfully happy. Ross was sweet to her during the day, and madly passionate every night. With each passing day she became more and more convinced that he loved her, despite his never saying so. Her own love for him was also growing stronger as she discovered more about him.

Helga had been right when she'd said they had similar personalities. They also had similar likes and dislikes in regard to just about everything. They were both mad about travel and Tennessee Williams's plays and the Beatles and playing cards, especially Five Hundred. It was uncanny. With Earl, she had had to pretend to like what he liked, just to keep him happy. With Ross, there was no pretending. Ever. She'd never felt so at one with a person.

There was another matter that did wonders for her humour as well. She didn't have morning sickness any more. How wonderful it was to be able to wake and not have to run to the bathroom! Her appetite improved considerably once her stomach was more settled, which was just as well since Helga had decided she needed 'building up'.

Yes, Vivien couldn't have been happier. Even Oliver seemed a little better, though he still tired quickly. The couple of hours she sat with him each morning and afternoon were mostly spent with her reading aloud while he relaxed in his favourite armchair. Occasionally they watched a video which Ross brought out from town.

The only fly in the ointment was Gavin, who remained as sour and uncommunicative as ever. He'd hardly spoken a dozen words to Vivien since her arrival, but she refused to let his mood upset her new-found happiness.

He was only young, she reasoned. He would get over his love for this Becky girl, as Ross was obviously getting over his. Every now and then, Vivien found herself puzzling over exactly what sort of girl this Becky Macintosh was to command such devotion.

She found out on New Year's Eve.

Vivien had just finished her morning visit with Oliver. Ross and Gavin were out mending fences. She and Helga were sitting in the kitchen having a mug of tea together when suddenly they heard a screeching of brakes on the gravel driveway. Before they could do more than raise their eyebrows, a slender female figure in pale blue jeans and a blue checked shirt came racing into the kitchen, her long, straight blonde hair flying out behind.

'Where's Ross?' she demanded breathlessly of Helga.

'Down in the south paddocks, mending fences. What is it, Becky? What's happened?'

'There was a small grass fire on the other side of the river. Dad and I put it out, but not before the wind picked up and a few sparks jumped the river. Now the fire's growing again and heading straight for our best breeding sheep. I've rung the emergency bush-fire brigade number, but apparently all of the trucks are attending two other scrub fires. They said they'd send a few men along in a helicopter, one of those that can water-bomb the fire. The trouble is the only pilot available is a real rookie. I thought Ross might be able to help.'

'I'll contact him straight away,' Helga said briskly.

'They have a two-way radio with them. I won't be a moment. The gizmo's in the study. I'll send them straight over to your place.'

'Thanks, Helga, I'd better get back. Mum's in a panic. Not that the fire's anywhere near the house. But you know what she's like.'

'Can I help in any way?' Vivien offered. 'Maybe I could stay with your mother while you do what you have to do.'

Vivien found herself on the end of a long look from the loveliest blue eyes. There was no doubt about it. Becky had not been behind the door when God gave out looks. Though not striking, she had a fragile delicacy about her that would bring out the protective instinct in any man. Too bad they never saw the toughness behind those eyes.

'I presume you're Vivien,' she said drily.

Vivien stood up, her shoulders automatically squaring. 'Yes, I am.'

Those big blue eyes flicked over her face and figure before a rueful smile tugged at her pretty mouth. 'If I'd known the sort of competition I had, I would have given up sooner. What odds, I ask myself, of Ross meeting someone like you at that horrid ball? Still, I have more important things to do today than worry over the fickle finger of fate. Yes, you can come and hold Mum's hand. That'll free me to help outside.'

Helga bustled back into the kitchen just in time to be told Vivien was going with Becky. Oddly enough, the older woman didn't seem to think this at all strange. For all her earlier criticisms about the girl's behaviour with Ross, she seemed to like Becky.

It came to Vivien then that there was more worth in this girl than she'd previously believed. That was why Helga wanted her for Gavin—to put some fire in his belly. Becky had a positive attitude and energetic drive Vivien could only admire.

'So when are you and Ross getting married?' Becky enquired while she directed the jeep at a lurching speed down the dusty road that led back to the highway.

'I don't know,' came the truthful answer. 'He—er—hasn't asked me yet.'

Becky slanted a frowning glance her way. 'Hasn't asked you yet? That's odd. When he confessed to me that he'd fallen in love with someone else the night of the ball at Wallaby Creek, and that the girl in question was pregnant by him, I naturally thought you'd be married as quickly as possible.'

Vivien held her silence with great difficulty. Ross had said that? Back *then*? That meant he'd virtually fallen in love with her straight away.

Oh, my God, she groaned silently. My God...

Her heart squeezed tight at the thought of all she had put Ross through that night, especially making him tell her he loved her like that. It also leant an ironic and very heart-wrenching meaning to Ross's statement a few days ago that he had always known the girl he loved didn't love him back, but that didn't stop him loving her. Of course Vivien had thought he meant Becky. But he had meant herself!

Vivien felt like crying. If only she'd known. But, of course, why would he tell her? No man would, certainly not after that day when he'd followed her to Sydney, only to discover that he was the dead-ringer of her previous lover, the man she supposedly still loved. God, it was a wonder his love for her hadn't turned to hate then and there.

Maybe it almost had for a while, she realised, remembering the incident in the library.

But if only he had told her later that night that he loved her, instead of letting her think his feelings were only lust.

And what of you? a reproachful voice whispered. Have you told him you love him? Have you reassured the father of your child that your feelings for him are anything more than just sexual?

She almost cried out in dismay at her own stupidity.

Oh, Ross...darling...I'll tell you as soon as I can, she vowed silently.

'Of course I always knew he wasn't madly in love with me, or I with him,' Becky rattled on. 'But we go back a long way, Ross and I. Gavin too, for that matter. We've always been great mates, the three of us. We love each other, but I think it's been more of a friendship love than anything else To be honest, I wasn't at all desperate to go to bed with Ross. But then...I've never been desperate to go to bed with any man as yet.' She sighed heavily. 'Maybe I will one day, but something tells me I'm not a romantic at heart.'

Vivien only hesitated for a second. After all, nothing ventured, nothing gained. 'Has it ever occurred to you that you might have been looking for passion with the wrong brother?'

The jeep lurched to one side before Becky recovered. She darted Vivien a disbelieving glance. 'You're not serious!'

'Never been more serious. Helga says Gavin's crazy

about you. He was simply crushed by your intention to marry Ross.'

'*Really*?'

'Yes, really. He's been as miserable as sin lately because he thinks you're suffering from a broken heart. He blames me and Ross.'

'But...but if he loves me, the stupid man, why hasn't he said so? Why hasn't he *done* something?'

'Too shy.'

'Too *shy*? With *me*? That's ridiculous! Why, we've been skinny dipping together!'

'Not lately, I'll bet.'

'Well, no...'

'Perhaps you should suggest you do so again some time. See what happens.'

Becky looked over at Vivien, blue eyes widening. 'You city girls don't miss a trick, do you? Skinny dipping, eh? Yes, well, I—er—might suggest that some time, but I can't think about Gavin right now. I have a fire to help put out.'

They fell silent as Becky concentrated on her driving. Not a bad idea, Vivien thought, since the girl drove as she no doubt did most things—with a degree of wild recklessness. Or maybe all country people drove like that on the way to a fire. Whatever, Vivien was hanging on to the dashboard for dear life.

Ross and Gavin must have gone across land, picking up Stan and Dave on the way, for all four men arrived at the homestead simultaneously with Becky and Vivien. A plump, fluttery lady raced out to greet them all with hysteria not far away.

'Oh, thank God, thank God,' she kept saying.

'Now, now, Mrs Macintosh,' Ross returned, patting her hand. 'Calm down. The cavalry's here.'

He turned to give Vivien a questioning look, but she merely smiled, hugging to herself the wonderful knowledge of his love for her. Later today, she would tell him of her own love. Not only would she tell him, but she would show him.

'There's the helicopter!' Becky shouted, pointing to the horizon. 'It's a water-bombing helicopter,' she explained to Ross, 'but the pilot's not very experienced. Do you think you might be able to help him?'

'Sure. I haven't exactly done that kind of thing myself before, but it can't be too difficult.'

The dark grey helicopter landed in a cloud of dust, forestalling any further conversation. It was all business. A side-door slid back to reveal several men inside. Stan, Dave and Gavin piled in with them. Ross climbed in next to the pilot, shouting back to Becky to collect some cool drinks and to drive down in the jeep.

Becky didn't look at all impressed at being given such a tame job to do, but in the end she shrugged resignedly. Within minutes of the helicopter taking off, she'd successfully filled two cool boxes with ice and drinks, refusing to let Vivien help her carry them to the jeep.

'You shouldn't be carrying heavy things when you're in the family way,' she was told firmly.

'Where will they get the water from to bomb the fire with?' Vivien asked as Becky climbed in behind the wheel.

'The dam, I guess, though there isn't too much water in it. Maybe the river.'

Vivien frowned. 'But wouldn't that be dangerous? The

river's not very wide and there are trees all along the
bank.'

'*Dangerous*? For the legendary Ross Everton?' Becky
laughed.

'I've heard him called that before, but I don't know
what it means.'

'It means, duckie, that you've got yourself hooked to
the craziest, most thrilling-seeking chopper cowboy that
ever drew breath. Ross prides himself on being able to fly
down and hover low enough to open gates by leaning out
of the cockpit. He'll heli-muster anything that moves in
any kind of country, no matter how rough and wild.
Cattle. Brumbies. Buffalo. He's a legend all over the outback for his skill and daring.' She gave Vivien a wry look
as she fired the engine. 'Having second thoughts, are we?'

'Of course not!' she returned stalwartly, and waved
Becky off.

But a type of fear had gripped her heart. Ross might
be very skilled, but hadn't he just admitted he hadn't done
this kind of job before? What if he made a mistake? What
if the helicopter crashed?

Vivien felt sicker than she ever had with morning sickness. She felt even sicker an hour later while she and Mrs
Macintosh stood together on the back veranda of the
homestead, from where they had a first-class view of what
was going on, both in the far paddocks and in the air. The
helicopter had indeed scooped up a couple of loads of
water from the dam, but clearly not enough. The grass fire
was still growing. Now, the helicopter was being angled
around to head for the river. Vivien just knew who it was
at the controls.

'Oh, God, no,' she groaned when the machine skimmed

the tops of trees in its descent to the narrow strip of water below.

She watched with growing horror when the helicopter dipped dangerously to fill the canvas bag, the rotor blades almost touching the surface of the water before the craft straightened and scooped upwards. 'I can't watch any more,' she muttered under her breath.

But she did, her heart aching inside her constricted chest as she watched Ross make trip after dangerous trip to that river then back to the fire. At last, the flames died, leaving nothing but a cloud of black smoke. Mrs Macintosh turned to hug her when, even from that distance, they heard the men's shouts of triumph.

Vivien couldn't feel total triumph, however. Fear was still gripping her heart. How could she bear Ross doing this kind of thing for a living? How could she cope with the continuous worrying? She wanted the father of her baby around and active when their child grew up. Not dead, or a paraplegic.

Her fears were compounded when the men came back to the house and Ross was laughing—actually laughing!—as the rookie pilot relayed tales of near-missed fences and trees. In the end, she couldn't bear it any more. She walked right up to him and said with a shaking voice, 'You might think that risking your life is funny, but I don't. I've been worried sick all afternoon, and I…I…' Tears flooded her eyes. Her shoulders began to shake.

Ross gathered her against his dusty chest. 'Hush. I'm all right, darling. Don't cry now…' He led her away from the others before tipping her tear-stained face up to him. 'Dare I hope this means what I think it means?'

'Oh, Ross, I love you so much,' she cried. 'I can't bear

to think of you risking your life every day. Don't ever go
back to doing that helicopter business. Please. I couldn't
bear it if you had an accident.'

'I won't have an accident.'

'You don't know that. You're not immortal. Or infallible. No one is. If you love me even a little—'

'A *little*? My God, Vivien, I *adore* you, don't you know
that?'

She stared up at him, stunned, despite what Becky had
told her. It sounded so much more incredibly wonderful
coming from Ross's actual lips. 'You...you've never actually told me,' she choked out. 'Not in words.'

'Well, I'm telling you now. I've loved you since the
first moment I set eyes on you, looking at me across that
crowded ballroom. You mean the world to me. But you
don't understand. I won't have an accident because—'

Mr Macintosh's tapping him on the shoulder interrupted what Ross was going to say.

'Ross...'

Ross turned. 'Yes?'

'Er—Helga just called. I'm sorry, but I have some bad
news.'

'Bad news?'

'Yes...your father...'

Vivien closed her eyes as a wave of anguish washed
through her, for she knew exactly what the man was going
to say. Fresh tears flowed, tears for the man who'd become her friend. More tears for the man she loved. He
was going to take this hard.

Mr Macintosh cleared his throat. 'He...he passed
away...this afternoon. I'm so sorry, lad.'

Ross's hold tightened around Vivien. Yet when he

spoke, his voice sounded calm. Only Vivien could feel him shaking inside. 'It's all right. Dad's dearest wish was that he would die at Mountainview. He...he's probably quite happy.'

Oliver Everton was cremated, in keeping with his wishes, and his ashes sprinkled over the paddocks of his beloved Mountainview. They had a large wake for him at the house, again in keeping with his wishes, and it was towards the end of this wake that Mr Parkinson, Oliver's solicitor, called the main beneficiaries of his will into the study.

Mr Parkinson sat behind the huge walnut desk while Ross and Vivien, Helga and Gavin pulled up chairs. Vivien was perplexed—and a little worried—over what she was doing there. If she was to be a beneficiary, that meant Oliver had changed his will recently. She was suddenly alarmed at what she was about to hear.

'I won't beat about the bush,' Mr Parkinson started. 'It appears that Oliver saw fit to write a new will a couple of days ago without consulting me. Oh, it's all legal and above-board, witnessed by Stan and Dave. Helga had it in her safe keeping...'

Vivien stared at Helga, who kept a dead-pan face.

'But I have to admit that the contents came as a shock to me. I think they might come as a shock to you too, Ross.'

Vivien finally dared to look at Ross, who didn't look at all worried. It crossed her mind then that he knew full well what was in that will. She went cold with apprehension.

'Aside from Ross being left a couple of real estate prop-

erties around Sydney and Helga being left a pension trust
fund to ensure she won't want for money for the rest of
her life, it seems that Oliver has left the bulk of his estate,
including the property Mountainview and all it contains,
to his second son, Gavin.'

Gavin sat bolt upright in his chair, clearly stunned. 'But
that's not fair. Mountainview is worth millions! *Ross...*'
He swivelled to throw a distressed look at his brother.
'You must know...I had no hand in this.'

'I know that,' Ross replied equably. 'Dad told me what
he was going to do. I fully agreed with his decision.'

Vivien almost gasped at his obvious twisting of the
truth. It had been Ross, she realised, who had insisted on
the change of will. This was what he had gone to see his
father about a few days ago, before it was too late. He
knew his father had actually left control of Mountainview
to *him*. He had sacrificed his inheritance for love of his
brother, for he knew his brother needed it more than he
did, in more ways than one.

Gavin was looking even more stunned. 'You *agreed*
with my having Mountainview?'

'Yes. I've been made an excellent offer for my fleet of
helicopters and the goodwill of my business. I'm going to
take it. Believe me, Gavin, I won't be wanting for a bob,
if that's what's worrying you. And don't forget about
those Sydney properties Dad left me.'

'But they'd be nothing compared to Mountainview!'

'That depends on the point of view. One of them is that
penthouse unit at Double Bay Mum inherited. It's hardly
worth peanuts. The other is a substantial acreage Dad
bought years ago just outside Sydney on the Nepean
River. I've always had a dream to set up an Australian

tourist resort, catering for people who want to experience typical Australian country life without having to actually travel out there. That piece of land on the Nepean would be the ideal site.'

'You've never mentioned this before,' Gavin said, clearly still worried.

Ross gave him a ruefully affectionate smile. 'We don't always talk about our dreams out loud, do we, little brother? I thought my duty lay here till I saw you had more heart for this place than I ever would.'

'And what will this tourist resort have in it, Ross?' Vivien joined in, intrigued by the thought of it all.

Smiling widely, he turned to her. 'Lots of things. There'll be a miniature farm with examples of all our animals, shearing exhibitions, sheep-dog trials. Individual cabins for people to stay in. Restaurants that serve typical Australian food. Barbecue and picnic facilities. Souvenir shops. All sorts of things. I think it could be a great success, especially if my wife joins in and helps me. She's a whiz with people...'

She stared back at him, having only heard the word—'wife'. He bent over and kissed her before turning back to face his brother.

'So don't worry about Dad leaving you Mountainview, Gavin. He's put it in the best of hands. And I think there might be a girl somewhere around here who might like to help you and Helga look after the place.'

'Gosh, I don't know what to say.'

Neither did Helga, it seemed. Tears were streaming down her face.

Vivien reached out to take Ross's hand. 'You are a

wonderful, wonderful man,' she murmured. 'Do you know that?'

'Yes,' he said, and leant close. 'You will marry me, won't you?'

'You know I will.'

'That's what your mother told me that day. She said if I were patient you'd come around. She said you loved me, but you just didn't know it yet.'

Vivien was astonished. 'Mum said that?'

'Sure thing. She told me her daughter didn't go round having babies with men she didn't love. I should have believed her sooner.'

A lump filled Vivien's throat. Dear heaven…her mother knew her better than she knew herself. But she'd been so right. So very right.

Mr Parkinson coughed noisily till they were all paying attention to him again. 'I have one more bequest to read out. It seems the late Mrs Everton had a sizeable amount of very valuable jewellery which has been kept in a bank vault in Sydney all these years. Mr Everton senior left it all to the mother of his first grandchild, Miss Vivien Roberts. To be worn, his will states. Not locked away. He says it could only be enhanced by Miss Roberts's beauty.'

Vivien tried not to cry, but it was a futile exercise. The tears had already been hovering. She began to sob quietly, Ross putting an arm round her shoulder to try and comfort her. Helga stood up abruptly and left the room, returning quickly with a tray full of drinks. She passed them all around.

'I wish to propose a toast to my employer and friend, Oliver Everton.'

They all stood up.

'May I?' Ross asked thickly.

Helga nodded.

'To Oliver Everton,' he said. 'He was a good father and a good friend. He was a good man. They don't come along like him too often...'

CHAPTER FOURTEEN

'IRVING! What do you think you're doing?' Vivien remonstrated. 'I asked you to film just the christening, but you've been following me around all afternoon with that darned camera. I came out here on my own back patio to catch a breath of fresh air and up you pop like a bad penny.'

Irving continued filming as he spoke. 'Now, Viv, sweetie, I don't often have such a gorgeous-looking subject to film. You're looking ravishing today in that white dress, especially with that pearl choker round your lovely neck. Have pity on me. I've been doing nothing but film sour old politicians for the channel lately. Of course, if a certain lady journalist would heed her old boss's pleas to return to work then I might get assigned some more interesting jobs...like that one out at Wallaby Creek.'

Vivien's laughter was dry. 'Mervyn can beg till he's blue in the face. I have no intention of ever returning to work for a man who's so stupid. Fancy keeping Bob on instead of me. No intelligence at all.'

'Didn't I tell you? Bob's moved to Western Australia. He's decided the politicians are more interesting over there.'

'Oh, so that's it! Now Mervyn has a hole in his staff and he thinks he can fill it with yours truly. No way, José. I'm very happy helping Ross build this place.' And she swept an arm round to indicate the mushrooming complex. Already their own house was finished on a spot overlooking the river. So was the gardener's cottage. The foundations of the restaurant and shops had been poured that week.

'That's what I told him,' Irving said. 'But he's a stubborn man.'

'Who's a stubborn man?' Ross remarked on joining them. Vivien thought he looked heart-stoppingly handsome in a new dark grey suit. And very proud, with his six-week-old baby son in his arms.

'Mervyn,' she explained. 'You know he keeps asking me to go back to work for him.'

'Why don't you?'

Vivien blinked at her husband. 'But you said—'

Ross shrugged. 'I always believe in letting people do what they want to do, regardless. If you're missing work then by all means go back. You know your mother's dying to get her hands on Luke here, and since your father agreed to quit the railways and take on the job as chief gardener you've got a built-in baby-sitter. Your parents will be living only a hundred yards away.'

Vivien could hardly believe her ears. That was one aspect of Ross's character that never ceased to amaze her: his totally selfless generosity. So different to Earl, who'd been greedily possessive of her time. He'd hated her working.

Thinking about the differences between Ross and Earl brought a small smile to her lips, for they were more different now than ever. Her mother had shown her a picture in a women's magazine the other day, of a couple at the Flemington races. Vivien had not recognised the man till she'd read the caption below the photograph:

Mr and Mrs Earl Fotheringham enjoying a day at the races.

She had stared at the photograph again, then had difficulty suppressing a burst of laughter. For Earl was not only grossly overweight, but he was going bald. In less than a year, he looked ten years older, and nothing like Ross at all. She'd shown the picture to Ross, who'd looked at it, then stared at her.

'And *this* is who I'm supposed to look like?' he said.

'Once upon a time,' she said, trying to keep a straight face.

When Ross had burst out laughing she had too. But from relief, rather than any form of mockery, for now Ross could put Earl's ghost to rest once and for all.

Vivien's father opened the sliding glass doors and popped his head out. 'Is this a private session, or can anyone join in?'

'By all means join us, Lionel,' Ross said warmly. 'Get Peggy out here too and we can have a family shot.'

Lionel looked sheepish. 'Well, actually I was told to bring you all back inside. Your mother says it's getting late, Vivien, and you should be opening the baby's presents.'

They all were soon gathered in the large living area of the modern, airy house, Vivien sitting down on the white leather sofa to begin opening the gifts and cards that were piled high on the coffee-table, while everyone looked on. Irving kept happily filming away. Vivien decided to ignore him as best she could, and began ripping off paper with relish.

There were all the usual christening presents from toys to teddies, clothes to engraved cups, all beautiful and much gushed over by everyone. Gavin, who had become ecstatically engaged to Becky the previous month, had already sent down their excuses at not being able to attend, since they were in the middle of shearing. He'd posted down the cutest toy lamb Vivien had ever seen. The card attached had a small note from Becky.

'What does she mean,' Ross asked, 'about how she's been practising her swimming a lot lately?'

Vivien felt her lips twitching. 'I—er—told her the only way to get good at anything was to practise it.'

Ross frowned. 'Becky practising swimming? That's silly. She's a fantastic swimmer. Why, we used to go...' His voice trailed off as suspicion dawned in his eyes. He gave Vivien a narrow-eyed stare. She busied herself with another present by way of distraction.

'Here's one from Helga,' she announced, feeling it all over before opening it. 'I wonder what it is.' It was quite bulky, but soft.

Ross groaned. 'I have an awful feeling of premonition that Helga's been knitting again.'

Vivien ripped the paper off and everyone just stared. It was, she supposed, a rug of some sort, knitted in the most ghastly combination of colours she had ever seen, not to mention different ply wools. Now she knew why Ross's jumpers had never seen the light of day. Who would think to combine mauve with orange with black with red with purple in a series of striped and checked squares that had no regular pattern? On the card was the following explanation:

I began this before I knew whether your baby would be a boy or a girl, so I decided that neutral colours would be best.

These were *neutral* colours? Vivien stared down at the rug, unable to think of a thing to say.

'What…what is it?' Vivien's mother finally asked.

'A horse blanket,' Ross stated with a superbly straight face. 'For Luke's first pony. Helga's horse blankets are quite famous. Horses love them.'

'Oh,' Peggy said.

'We'll put it in a drawer for him, sweetheart,' Ross said to Vivien. 'Perhaps we should put a special drawer aside in which to save up all of Helga's marvellous gifts.'

'Yes, dear,' she returned with an even better poker-face. 'I think that would be best.'

They were lying in bed that night after Luke had finally condescended to go to sleep, chuckling over the incident.

'I almost died when I first saw it,' Vivien giggled.

'Don't you mean ''almost died laughing''? And now, madam, would you like to tell me in the privacy of our bedroom what decadent advice you gave Becky?'

'Decadent advice? Who, me?'

'Yes, *you*, city broad.'

She laughed. 'That's for me to know and you to find out.'

'I think I already have…'

'Then why are you asking? Besides, it worked, didn't it? They're engaged and happy.'

'Not as happy as we are,' Ross insisted, pulling her close.

Vivien lifted her mouth to his in a tender kiss. 'No one's as happy as we are.'

'Too true.'

'Which is why I'm not going back to work.'

'You're not?'

'No. I'm happy doing what I'm doing, looking after Luke and helping you. Maybe some day I might want to go back to television, but not right now. I want to be right here when Luke cuts his first tooth, says his first word, takes his first step. Let Mervyn find someone else,' she went on without any regret. 'I can see I'm not going to be available for at least ten years, till our last child has gone to school.'

Startled, Ross propped himself up on his elbow and stared down at her. 'Our *last* child? How many are we going to have, for heaven's sake?'

'Oh, at least four. Kids these days need brothers and sisters to stick up for them. It's a tough world.'

He shook his head in a type of awed bewilderment. 'You never cease to amaze me, Mrs Everton. First, you bravely went ahead and had my baby when most women in your shoes wouldn't have. Now, after you've just been through a rotten long labour, you tell me you want a whole lot more! I'm beginning to wonder if you're a glutton for punishment or just plain crazy.'

'I'm crazy,' she said, and with a soft, sexy laugh pulled him down into her arms. 'Crazy about you...'

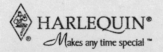

If you enjoyed what you just read,
then we've got an offer you can't resist!

Take 2 bestselling love stories FREE!

Plus get a FREE surprise gift!

Clip this page and mail it to Harlequin Reader Service®

IN U.S.A.	**IN CANADA**
3010 Walden Ave.	P.O. Box 609
P.O. Box 1867	Fort Erie, Ontario
Buffalo, N.Y. 14240-1867	L2A 5X3

YES! Please send me 2 free Harlequin Presents® novels and my free surprise gift. Then send me 6 brand-new novels every month, which I will receive months before they're available in stores. In the U.S.A., bill me at the bargain price of $3.12 plus 25¢ delivery per book and applicable sales tax, if any*. In Canada, bill me at the bargain price of $3.49 plus 25¢ delivery per book and applicable taxes**. That's the complete price and a savings of over 10% off the cover prices—what a great deal! I understand that accepting the 2 free books and gift places me under no obligation ever to buy any books. I can always return a shipment and cancel at any time. Even if I never buy another book from Harlequin, the 2 free books and gift are mine to keep forever. So why not take us up on our invitation. You'll be glad you did!

106 HEN CNER
306 HEN CNES

Name	(PLEASE PRINT)
Address	Apt.#
City	State/Prov.	Zip/Postal Code

* Terms and prices subject to change without notice. Sales tax applicable in N.Y.
** Canadian residents will be charged applicable provincial taxes and GST.
  All orders subject to approval. Offer limited to one per household.
  ® are registered trademarks of Harlequin Enterprises Limited.

HARLEQUIN®
SUPERROMANCE

Due to popular reader demand,
Harlequin Superromance® is expanding
from 4 to 6 titles per month!

Starting May 1999, you can have more
of the kind of stories that you love!

- Longer,
  more complex
  plots
- Popular themes
- Lots of
  characters
- A great
  romance!

*Available May 1999
at your favorite retail outlet.*

HARLEQUIN®
Makes any time special ™

THE AUSTRALIANS

**The Wonder from Down Under:
where spirited women win the hearts
of Australia's most independent men!**

If you missed any of the books in **The Australians** series,
act now to order your copy today!

The Australians